SPECIAL OFFER

Stories by Jerry Bumpus

Carpenter Press

Published by:

CARPENTER PRESS
ROUTE 4
POMEROY
OHIO 45769

LIBRARY OF CONGRESS CATALOGUING IN PUBLICATION DATA

Bumpus, Jerry.
Special Offer.

CONTENTS: The angel business.—House-hunting near the frontier —The love of beasts. (etc.)

I. Title
PS 3552.U464S67 813.54 80-20671
ISBN 0-914140-08-6

Publication of this book was supported by a grant from the National Endowment for the Arts, a federal agency in Washington, D.C.

MEMBER
COSMEP
COMMITTEE OF SMALL MAGAZINE
EDITORS AND PUBLISHERS
BOX 703 SAN FRANCISCO, CA 94101

The stories in this collection originally appeared, sometimes with different endings, as follows: "Special Offer," *Seneca Review*; "The Angel Business," *Kansas Quarterly*; "The Love of Beasts," *X-1*, a collection of experimental fiction published by The Smith Press; "With the Mory Bot," *Ampersand Magazine*; "Mr. Spoon's Visit," *Prism International*; "A Very Modern Home," *Quartet*; "Pizeop," *Texas Quarterly*; "Mrs. Bell and Her Dog," *Red Clay Reader*, (also anthologized in *Cutting Edges*); "The Fudgers," *Story Quarterly*; "On the Emperor's Birthday," *Mississippi Review*. The author is grateful to the editors for permission to reprint.

CONTENTS

Illustration by David Lynas

for Bettie

SPECIAL OFFER

The huge new building ten miles outside town resembled a hangar, with its arching roof, except where the hangar door should have been two show windows yawned up the hill toward the highway. A truck with a crane lifted a sign above the windows and when it was turned on it explained in red neon ***Furniture***. "Well? How's that?" asked the fellow from the sign company. The man who bought the sign nodded and walked into the building and switched it off.

People drove out from town and looked down from the highway at the dark windows and the unlighted sign which appeared to have already begun rusting. "Um. Not open for business yet"—and they would drive by. But now and then a light could be seen burning at the rear of the building; inevitably someone, seeing the light, drove down into the parking lot, got out of his car, and went up to one of the big plate glass windows. Framing his hands to his face, he put his head to the window. At the rear of the store he saw a man sitting in a kitchen chair with a lamp shining over his shoulder, reading.

Then one fall morning a procession of semi-trailers lumbered down from the highway onto the store's parking lot. A band of silent men in gray overalls unloaded furniture as fast as they could—while the big trucks' idling engines coughed and gabbled.

Now when the curious came out from town they found the neon sign still wasn't burning, and the lights inside weren't on, but when they went to the windows they saw the place was full of furniture. And the front door wasn't locked.

Someone opened the door and went in. Others followed but hesitantly, glancing around nervously. They made as if to look at the furniture.

No price tags were attached to the chairs, the tables, the sofas, and in the darkness it was hard to tell much about the quality of the furniture, especially the farther one went into the building; only a few went clear to the back, and it was really quite pointless, for they could see absolutely nothing, and ended up merely feeling their way from sofa to sofa in the dark.

During the first week, the customers usually couldn't find the owner and had to do their best on their own. When they did happen upon him he would be sitting in a recliner near the front of the store with a book in his hands. Often the customers passed right by, not noticing him. Or those who did, would stand looking at him: because he was so perfectly motionless, they took him for a mannequin, and passed without speaking. The few truly keen observers saw the subtle rise and fall of his breathing and they would lean down, putting their faces in his, and speak directly into him: usually something like, "Hey!" or "Whacha doin'?"

He would close his book, smile wanly, and rising, show these customers about, even going so far as to offer a word or two of salesmanship: "Now here we have a chair"—poking the cushion. "Soft, eh?" The customers would take turns sitting in the chair, leaning back, turning their heads from side to side as people do when trying to decide if they are truly comfortable; they would look blankly up at their companions and at the man showing them the furniture. "There you are. Eh?" the man would say, and they would nod vaguely.

He would move them along. "Now here we have a dining room table." The customers circled the table. "You, here," he said, guiding the husband to the head of the table. "Now." The customers pulled out the chairs and sat at the table. "There you are again. Eh?"

Winter settled in. As the days grew darker the owner moved farther and farther to the front of the store, until at last he sat hour after hour in the front window, but it didn't matter that now customers could have easily spotted him and enlisted his assistance in looking about, for people no longer came out to the store. Driving by on the highway they didn't even slow and look down the hill at the store.

So the owner of the store was sitting in the window, looking over the top of the book he held, when the first snow of winter came. It brought to an end that particular gray November day—or at least brought the light to an end.

A pick-up truck pulls off the highway and slices the snow in the parking lot with black lines. The truck is an extraordinary, menacing purple; the smooth hood and fenders pulsate under their tight radiant skin. Large chromium coils like erupting intestines curl down from the hood and end in exhaust pipes. The windshield is trimmed in reddish brown fur, as is the entire cab, in which the seats are shaped so the driver and his passenger don't sit but sprawl, tilting back so far they must crane their necks to see down and out the windshield. The truck rumbles across the parking lot and stops with its front bumper touching one of the huge plate glass windows.

The driver's door, on which is painted in black Gothic letters ***Candyman***, opens and out climbs a young man with coarse black hair framing his oblong, wide-mouthed, flat and wide-nostriled nose, and eyes which sag, droop downward, the corners of his eyes parallel above the pupils of his eyes; his eyes appear melting toward his mouth. His lips are thick as thumbs. From a gold ring in the lobe of one ear hangs a delicate purple penis with precise rhinestone testicles.

Out of the other door, on which is painted ***Daisy***, climbs a gaunt round-shouldered girl with orange hair radiating from her head like a halo. She can barely move her legs. Takes short, hobbling steps—either her jeans are so tight they bind her like iron, or maybe its worse than that, she is in pain! Suffering from a disease that affects her joints and bones. Or the malady is centered between her legs: she walks bent forward in the manner of a person exaggeratedly, comically—and belatedly—protecting her virtue. Her face, beneath its great bright blossom of hair, is still and small as a doll's, though it doesn't have the shininess of a doll's: it is dark gray and the small nose and cheeks, the small round chin, have the lumpiness of features briskly pinched from clay. It is a face for which expressions would be difficult, if not impossible—except the avid, big-eyed, undeniably simian directness of expression which is on her face now. As she follows the young man to the door of the furniture store, she leans even farther forward, stumbling in the snow-covered gravel in her cowboy boots, her leather jacket open and exposing her luminous green blouse and her breasts big as men's heads.

The young man opens the front door and he and the girl stand looking across the mounds and shadows of furniture. "Gee, Candyman," she says in a tight, piping voice like those incredible beings one hears when a recorder runs backwards. "Far out!"

Candyman starts down the aisle of furniture with Daisy behind him. They walk quickly, their footsteps muffled by the thick carpet—and they walk even faster until they break into a run. They run up and down the aisles, jumping on the furniture, bouncing from sofa to sofa.

"Hey!" Candyman shouts, his voice hoarse and flat. "Give it to me." Entranced, he stands eyes closed, head back, hands raised as if stopping everything. Daisy flings off her jacket, tears off her blouse, baring those pale bomb-nosed breasts blurred with bruised, with mauled nipples swollen big as apples. She shucks off her jeans, boots. Last, she flings off her hair, sending the orange wig sailing over two rows of sofas; under it she's bald as an egg, intensifyting the features of her face, the eyes, nose, the lips clenching as she rushes to Candyman and rips open his belt and unbuttons his jeans and pulls them down. Then she pivots, bends down, and backs against him. Her face grits tighter as she struggles, on her toes, bucking and twisting about, her hands on her knees. Then—"Eee!" Her eyes pop open and her face expands in an expression that is both amazed and oddly pensive.

"Go!" Candyman yells.

Daisy rigidly convulses, her entire body quivering as if electrified, and this reverberates to Candyman, setting him a-quiver as well, though the energy of movement is absorbed before it reaches his face which is intent and immobile as he stares across the furniture.

"Whoee," Candyman slowly, mournfully calls. "Uuuooee. Who oh, whoee."

Daisy's shaking ceases after ten or fifteen minutes, and they stand there breathing. Then she moves forward, straightens as much as she can—though she is still bent—and turns to Candyman whose eyes are closed, his nostrils big as the twin barrels of a double-barreled shotgun, breathing deeply. Daisy pulls up his jeans, and with both hands tucks in his member which stares down at the floor like a salmon.

Daisy then plops cross-legged on the floor and slumps forward, breathing with a whistling wheeze, her bony shoulders shaking. When she recovers she reaches over, picks up her jeans. She tilts onto her back and with her legs straight up, pulls the jeans on one leg, then the other. She gets to her feet and picks up her blouse and puts it on. She pauses for breath, then carefully buttons the blouse. She puts on her jacket, then goes around looking for her wig. She finds it under a sofa and carrying it in her hand, follows Candyman as they continue their tour of the store.

They, like most others, stop and squint into the darkness at the rear of the store. They then turn and wander toward the front.

*

It was easy to find their home. The purple pick-up could be seen from the town square down one of the side streets. It was parked in front of the house.

The snow was melting as soon as it touched the front yard. Consequently the yard was a gread mudwallow where a doorless, windowless car nosed into the earth, its rear wheels in the air. Parts of cars were sinking in various angles and poses of half-burial: rusty wheels arched in the mud like ruined rainbows; headlights stared up from the mud at the sky; a grille with some teeth missing grinned out from under the porch. A steering wheel was looped over the stubby black chimney pipe sticking from the roof.

The house itself was a cardboard furniture crate covered with tan imitation brick. The small windows weren't curtained or shaded, but didn't need to be: they were blind with the sky's reflection.

He stepped carefully onto the porch and tapped with his fingernails on the soft door. It opened a crack and Candyman looked out.

"I'm E. Joe Fine. From the furniture store." He smiled.

The door shut. From inside Joe Fine heard an up and down mumbling as if several people were humming. The door opened and there were Candyman and Daisy wearing their jackets, jeans, and boots. In the dark house Daisy's orange hair seemed to be the only illumination.

"Thank you," Joe Fine said and stepped through the door. The room was very small: as Candyman shut the door behind Joe Fine, the three of them touched down the lengths of their bodies, bumping hips and pressing together as they turned to maneuver the shutting of the door, and Joe Fine smiled widely, then laughed sharply. "We're dancing," he said in Candyman's face, then grinned in Daisy's.

"Huh?" she said, her gray lips parting.

"May I have a seat?" Joe Fine said. "To explain?"

"Yeah. Sure," Candyman said and nodded to the wall.

Glancing over his shoulder Joe Fine saw boards nailed to the walls as benches. He sat down on one. The young people sat on the bench across the room from him, their knees interlocking with his. "Now," he said. "I'm E. Joe Fine and as you know I have a furniture store on the highway."

They stared at him.

"And you're Candyman, and you're Daisy," Joe Fine said.

They nodded.

"Good. Now. I saw you in my store recently. Customers." Joe Fine began to cross his legs. This became complicated and took a great deal of doing both on his part and on the part of Candyman and Daisy who had to turn sideways on their bench, lift and turn their legs to accommodate Joe Fine's. "I was wondering if something is the matter." He waited, but they didn't answer. "I mean, you came in and looked . . . and left. I was expecting you again, first thing this morning. And I find you just sitting here."

"Well . . ." Candyman said and as the word finished, his mouth hung open. His big tongue moved forward as if coming to take a look out; his mouth shut, wary of the tongue's tricks.

"I hope you don't plan to take your business elsewhere," Joe Fine said.

"Huh?" Candyman said.

"I hope you aren't going to another store today. Are you?"

"Oh," Candyman said. "Uh smatter fack, yeah."

"We're going to the Star," Daisy said. Her voice sounded as if she were swiftly skidding backwards into the infinite space stacked directly behind her. It was a wire voice, her words vibrating inside themselves, *ing, ing*.

"The Star?" Joe Fine said.

"Yeah," Candyman said. "On Third Street. We go up in the balcony."

Joe Fine closed his eyes and saw the theater, green and yellow, crumbling, with sagging balcony and forward-tilting seats, shredded cushions, the ancient wooden floor coated with a carpet of condoms, slippery as banana peels. As Joe Fine watched, the shadows of the balcony wimpled, a slow overlapping and underturning of groaning darkness.

"Then you're no longer interested in furniture?" Joe Fine said.

They stared down at the tangle of legs. "I guess not," Candyman said.

"Too bad," Joe Fine said."I was about to run a special offer."

They looked up.

"It's aimed at people just like you." Joe Fine looked down at his small white hands. Then he chuckled. Looked up with a crafty, complicated smile. The smile of success. "I can't be dishonest," he said smoothly. "It's not my nature. I gotta be open. With everybody. Especially with you.

"What I'm saying, Candyman," he said, leaning forward and putting his hand on Candyman's thigh just south of the great lump that extended down his leg, "this offer is special for you and your lady fair. In fact it's just for you."

His voice lowered confidentially and he said in a deep, manly tone, "To level with you, if you guys don't come back to my store, the whole business is ruined. See? So I *got* to make this special offer. Without you, there's virtually nothing."

He leaned back, folded his hands on his lap. "Think it over a minute or two."

Candyman and Daisy looked at each other, then back at him. "What? . . ."

Joe Fine smiled. "Look at it this way. What have you got here? A nice place. Sure it's small, but nice. The right thing for love birds starting out on life's journey. But you want more, eh? Sure. Everybody wants more. Look." From inside his jacket Joe Fine took a heavy metal badge. Standing, he reached over and stuck it to the wall at the far end of the room. Within the bright red rim of the badge a yellow spiral centered on a ball bearing painted blue. "There," Joe Fine said. "It's a start. Little things help a place. See how it is? Make your life a little fresher. You know? Now.

"I level with you because you're sweet kids and I like you. You got to get started, young man. And you—"pointing a finger at Daisy's tiny face—"you got to start thinking too, eh?

"Which brings us back to my offer. This is it." He lifted both arms, spread them wide, reaching up to the ceiling as if to adjust it. He slowly brought his arms down, his eyes closed. "You two people's my future. I know it, now you know it too. Without you both, I'm owl shit.

"So you got to be there tomorrow morning. At nine sharp. From then on, every day. And what'll it do for you?"—he opened his eyes, arching his forehead in great furrows. "Everything. Because," he whispered, "it's the big business. See? The *big* business."

They nodded. "But . . ." Candyman said.

"What's this? Doubts?"

Candyman shook his head slowly. "I guess not."

"Good." Joe Fine stood. "Til tomorrow," and he struggled his way from the tangle of legs and went out the door.

The next morning Joe Fine could barely see the pick-up through the blizzard as it turned off the highway and pushed through the deep snow on the lot. When they came in the front door, stomping the snow off their boots and beating it off their shoulders, Joe Fine went forward and said, "You're the cream of the crop, you know what I mean?"

He led them to a dining table and sat them down. Reaching behind a sofa he produced a flash camera and took a shot. "This isn't why we're here," he said, waiting the sixty seconds, "but it gives us an idea of *where* we are, you know? He glanced at the camera and it answered with a strong clear beep so much like Daisy's voice she leaned forward and started moving her lips to catch up with herself.

Joe Fine pulled the picture out of the camera. "Well, now." He put it on the dining table for them to see. Their bodies had been cut off. "How you like it?" he said. Their heads in the picture were smiling in an odd gaping manner, showing their tongues and all their teeth; their eyes were too wide as if their heads were being blown up with air.

"So much for photography," Joe Fine said, tossing the camera and picture onto a sofa. "Allow me." He stepped behind Daisy, removed her jacket, and patted the bristly orange wig. She looked up at him, her rubbery face tight, as he went around and took off Candyman's jacket. He paused, looking at the earring hanging from Candyman's ear. "Hm." He popped it off and thumped it into the darkness of the furniture surrounding them.

"Uuyaa," Candyman said, his voice rising, and he started to turn and rise at the same time.

But Joe Fine had both hands on his shoulders, held him seated, and at the same time he spoke he pinched Candyman's ear lobe between thumb and forefinger. "*Trust* in me. There's more, you'll see, we've just begun."

He sat down on the edge of the table, his legs crossed casually, leaning on one hand and bending forward between Candyman and Daisy. "I suppose you're interested in money, eh? Everyone is, you know."

They nodded. A drop of blood fell from Candyman's ear and spattered softly on the table.

"Money," Joe Fine said. "All right. We'll start with that. How about fifty-three thousand? Like that, do you?"

"Gee, Candyman," Daisy said.

Candyman's mouth hung open. He frowned at Joe Fine. "Yeah."

"That's fifty-three thousand *each*. For you. And for you."

"Oh gee," she said.

"God," Candyman said.

"Now there are other things related to money. Okay? Cars. Motorcycles. Suede boots—black for you and white for you. With thick heels. Classy, eh? Now."

Joe Fine pushed himself off the table and unbuttoned his suit jacket. "Look at this." He opened it and showed them the lining—bright rippling red. "And feel this." He whipped out a large blue silk handkerchief and leaning forward rubbed Daisy's face with it as if he were wiping the rearview mirror on a car. "Eh?"

"Gee. Nice," she said and looked up at him intently.

"Stand up," he told Candyman. Candyman obeyed. "Let's see . . ." Joe Fine undid Candyman's belt and fly, and pushed down the jeans. "Huh?" Candyman said.

With both hands Joe Fine lifted Candyman's member and laid it on the table. Daisy stood and started taking off her jeans.

"Hold on!" Joe Fine said to her, not turning away from the member. "Now. Let's all of us think about this. What exactly *is* it?"

The four were so quiet they heard outside the store the snow falling decently and humbly.

"Let's just look and see," Joe Fine said. Reaching down he drew back the foreskin with both hands. The head of the member appeared, large and surprised. "Well, what have we here?" Joe Fine said as the member began to swell, extending across the table as if it would leave Candyman's body and crawl off into the furniture.

Daisy was making *eee* softly. "Hm?" Joe Fine said, glancing at her.

"Candyman has needs," Daisy said in her distinct piping voice.

Joe Fine nodded. "Indeed. Well." The member, having reached its full extent, hovered off the table, and Candyman leaned on his heels to counterpoise the weight.

"Oh," Daisy said, writhing where she sat. "Oh, oh."

"Hold off," Joe Fine commanded. "Watch this." Joe Fine arched his shoulders and eyebrows, bared his teeth, and extended a long-fingered cold white hand hypnotically in the direction of the member. Then he began breathing through his teeth with great intensity, and very slowly moved forward, the hand now shining like ice, coming nearer and nearer the swollen member which like a great confident lizard, waited, a big vein pulsing. The shining hand hovered inches from the member. The snow fell. They held their breath. He touched it.

And it shriveled.

Right into itself—not drawing back into Candyman, but shriveled at full length. As if all the blood in it was freezing or dehydrating. They could almost see the surprise in the expression on the member's mouth as it went down from being a third leg for Candyman, to being a precarious splinter of summer lightning sticking from his belly.

Then Joe Fine reached up near Candyman's fly and thumped the member, breaking it off an inch or so beyond the fly.

Daisy screamed.

"It's all right," Candyman said, his voice light and rather breathless, as if he had just climbed out of a swimming pool. "It doesn't hurt. Not at all."

"And how do you feel otherwise?" Joe Fine said, not looking at him.

"I guess I feel all right."

"Aiee. Aiee. Oh Jesus, aiee," Daisy said, jumping up and down and pulling with both hands at her breasts, her orange wig falling off the back of her head.

Joe Fine dived across the dining table and with his thumbs impaled Daisy's nostrils. He clamped his hands around her tiny head, swung her around, and banged her down on the table. She was kicking and fighting, striking Joe Fine with her fists. "Help me!" Joe Fine yelled, and Candyman rushed around and grabbed her wrists.

"There," Joe Fine said, and freeing one hand reached down and undid her jeans. He forced his hand between her legs.

"No, Jesus, no," Daisy screamed.

Joe Fine gritted his teeth, straining.

Then with a *plup* he pulled out a bright pink creature no bigger than a toad and shaped like a schmoo. He tossed it onto the dining table where it wobbled and swayed, then stood like a bowling pin. "There," Joe Fine said.

Daisy straightened up and looked at the schmoo in the center of the table. "That's . . . it?"

Joe Fine nodded, smiling.

"Well," Daisy said and put her hands to her face, smoothing back her cheeks from their intense frown, "it's certainly a surprise after all this time to see that it's actually just *that*."

Candyman had turned away and having found the clothes Joe Fine had brought, was putting them on. Daisy went off to the side and put on the dress she found on a sofa, and a blond wig.

They went to the front of the store and stood looking out at the blizzard. Beside them on the wall was the switch. Candyman reached over and turned it on.

The big red neon ***Furniture*** came on above the window, lighting the parking lot and the slanting snowflakes which seemed madly attracted to the red light.

It hadn't been on two minutes before a car, creeping along the highway in the storm, came to a stop: it was evidently searching for the buried driveway into the parking lot. "No," Daisy whispered. "Turn it off."

"If I do they won't . . ." Candyman said.

"That's all right," she said. "We don't want them down here."

"But . . ."

"That's not why this happened," Daisy said sternly. "This happened because . . ."

The car moved farther along, stopped, then backed up, still looking for the driveway. "Who are they?" she said.

"People," Candyman said.

"Should we?" she said, and now there was in her voice

something like ease, an opening to wide spaces, a softness that came from a mouth that was large and wide, capable of anything.

"Yes," Candyman said. "I really think we should. I really do. After all, that's what we're here for."

"Yes," she said and she laughed for the first time in her life. Turning, she saw the other switch, and she turned on the lights inside the store.

The furniture bludgeoned into life, great mounds of vinyl, wood, leather, all roaring in the store's silence, roaring for people.

THE ANGEL BUSINESS

One dark afternoon a taxi came down the road. I rose from my desk and went to the window. The car stopped and the driver, an old man, walked around and opened the back door.

A large man got out. When he had straightened to his full height, I recognized my old school chum, Russell. I could hardly believe my eyes.

We stood before the fire and toasted the past. Russell's hair was gray, but he was still robust. He talked loudly and often interrupted himself with braying laughter which rattled through the empty house. I told him I had given up. He seemed not to hear. He talked on, and his face relaxed—his forehead unwrinkled, and his cold blue eyes were as clear and intense as when we were boys. "To great things!" he shouted and struck his glass against mine, nearly shattering them. We drank. Then—"To success!" We drank.

"I say, Russell," I put in quickly, "what have you been doing all these years?"

He clenched his teeth. His face bloated. "A total waste. But I hunt. . ."

"And that's why you've come out here?"

Then he whispered, "There were business ventures."

"Tell me, " I said. "I'm quite interested."

He looked at me sharply. "You are? Why? You said you had given up. Anyway, *you* should know about failure."

"How did you know. Who told you?"

"It doesn't matter." He turned away. In a mirror across the room I saw his face dimly reflected. He was grinning hideously.

But when he turned again to me, his expression was blank. "Let's forget the past," he said calmly. "I am married. Did you know?"

"Of course not. Congratulations."

"Actually it's the second time. My first wife died."

"Oh. I'm sorry."

"Don't be. She didn't *die*. I killed her. Shot her with my bow and arrow."

He exploded with laughter and slapped me on the shoulder. "To the future!" he shouted.

We drank. "Will I have the pleasure of meeting the new Mrs. Russell?"

"By and by." His face sagged, darkened. It seemed tremendously thick, as if layered with clay. His eyes shifted beneath his brows. "I'm on to something," he whispered.

"Good." When he didn't go on, I added: "I will help if I can, if that's what you want. If it's a matter of money."

"You don't understand," he said darkly.

"What is it?"

"Angels."

"Oh. Angels?"

I waited. The pause lengthened: we faced each other, disappearing into ourselves in the fading light. "My good friend," I said, "please stay. I am glad you have come. You will find peace here, as I have. The solitude. . ."

A servant entered the room! The man arrogantly looked at me and announced dinner was served.

Russell laughed and pounded me on the back. "He's part of my staff," he said. "The others are on their way." He pointed to the window—the taxi was coming up the driveway. Through the darkness I saw the car was filled with shadows that could easily have been people.

In the dining room the long table was set for two. From the kitchen entered more servants, carrying trays.

One of them announced Mrs. Russell had arrived.

"Good," Russell said. He sat down and motioned for me to take the other place. I obeyed, and then asked, "Won't Mrs. Russell join us for dinner?"

Russell shook his head. "Let us save that for later, shall we?"

The servants' procession continued until the table was piled high with food.

We sat before the fire in the study. Perhaps this was the time: "Russell," I said, "I want to talk to you about my work here, why I have given up, why I have lived out here all these years. Surely you have wondered."

He leaned forward. "Ahh," he said.

But he wasn't looking at me. A figure in white emerged from the shadows. She was tall and thin, with orange hair standing on end. Her skin was milky white. A violet vein pulsed at her temple, and the same faint violet traced her throat.

She carried a little white ball. Looking at neither of us, she bit into it. A cookie! Slowly, meditatively, she ate it.

She brushed the crumbs from her fingertips and pulled a ribbon at her throat. Her gown dropped. The room was silent except for the pop and hiss of the fire. She knelt and bent forward onto her elbows.

A snort echoed in the room. Russell had stood and was taking off his trousers.

The next morning Russell came downstairs and cheerfully insisted I join him for breakfast.

"No, Russell," I said firmly.

"Oh, I say. You're embarrassed about last night." He brayed.

I refused to look at him.

"Come on, old fellow," he said. "You must eat. Even you eat." He linked his arm in mine and pulled me to the dining room.

"Today is the day!" he roared down the table at me.

When we finished, Russell's servants brought in heavy trousers, hunting jackets, and Russell's bow and arrows. We donned the hunting clothes and went outside where the taxi waited. The old man tipped his hat and opened the car door. Then above us a loud firm voice commanded: "Russell!"

"Yes, love," Russell answered. A huge woman stood on the balcony. She wore a green velvet dress with gold piping and black ruffles. Her face was deeply wrinkled, and her steep forehead was topped by a helmet of gray hair.

"Wait for Dr. Horace," she said.

"Very well. And you, my dear? Will you join us?"

She turned and went into the house.

"Who was that?" I asked.

"My wife. Pardon me for not introducing you."

Out of the house came a little man wearing a black top hat, black cape, black suit, and black patent leather slippers. Under his arm he cradled a shotgun. "Good morning," he said curtly, looking at neither of us. He went straight to the taxi and got into the back seat.

"This is Dr. Horace—Eunice's husband," Russell said.

"I believe you met my wife last night," the doctor said, looking at me.

"Shall we be off?" Russell said. He and I got in beside the driver.

We followed the dirt road into the woods. The farther we drove, the more worried I became about the shotgun. At last I glanced over my shoulder. . .

The little doctor was sprawled in the seat, knees wide apart. His head hung forward and his hat had fallen off, exposing a skull wisped with dull brown hair. His open cape and coat revealed his shirt, stained with blots of pale green, purple, and the same orange of Eunice's hair.

I leaned toward Russell. "Dr. Horace is having a nap."

Russell shook his head. "He swoons. It's the opium muffins. He and Eunice are devotees."

The road narrowed to a path, and the driver stopped the car. On the cold air floated the pellucid voices of birds.

Russell stalked through the woods. I followed, and behind me trailed Dr. Horace. As if charmed, animals came trotting straight to Russell, and he shot them with his bow. We dragged the dead beasts behind us.

Dr. Horace dropped farther back. The last time I looked over my shoulder, he was lying down in the leaves.

Late that afternoon when we returned, servants unloaded the game from the back seat of the taxi. They heaved out the stag, partridges, the boar, turkeys, hares, ducks, and the black bear onto the dusty ground. The pile stood higher than the taxi. I stuck my head into the car: the back seat was drenched with blood.

Russell and I went into the study and were having a drink when Mrs. Russell entered.

She stood a head taller than Russell and I—and that head was three hands wide, with a face chalk-white except for two red dots on her cheeks. Her eyes were nearly closed under thick eyelids as she spoke: "Professor Koch, his wife, and daughter have arrived."

Russell turned to me. A gloating smile came to his face and crept too far in both directions, revealing his jagged teeth. "My good man," he whispered, "I do hope you won't refuse us."

"Refuse you?"

"You have been awfully good so far."

"Feel quite free, Russell. But as for myself. . ." I turned away.

"No more of that!" he shouted. "Remember, I'm bringing you to life." He laughed loudly, his mouth wide.

Eight of us sat down to dinner: the Russells, Dr. Horace and Eunice, myself, and the Koch family—the Professor, bald, obese, perspiring; his small wife, constantly whispering to herself; and their adolescent daughter, skinny as a stick, her blue paper eyes staring across the table at Dr. Horace. The conversation turned to angels.

"I would like to believe you, Russell," Professor Koch said. "But you can't blame me for being skeptical."

Russell laughed, squinting intensely. "Skeptical! Wait until you see."

"See?" Koch said.

"Of course," Dr. Horace said. "We're quite prepared."

"Oh," Koch said to Dr. Horace. "You are Russell's colleague in this venture." Koch turned to me. "And you?"

I shook my head. "I know nothing of it."

"He hasn't asked you to invest?"

Russell interrupted: "I asked *no one* to invest." He glared at Mrs. Koch, busily whispering to herself—"Must you do that?"

She froze.

Russell went on: "I ask no one for money. Angels aren't impressed by money."

"Very well, Russell," Koch said, "let's get on with it."

As we were leaving the dining room, Koch's daughter caught my attention and with her lips silently enunciated *Wait*. The others went into the study. The girl sternly asked me, "Is it true about Mr. Russell?"

"Is what true? Frankly, I'm lost."

"Is it true he has powers?"

"Russell? Powers? Why, I. . ." I hurried past the girl when I realized that if I looked only a little deeper into the strange dry blue of her eyes I would make a horrible discovery.

The others sat in a half-circle facing Russell. We joined them. "Angels," Russell said.

Koch spoke: "Bona fide angels, or local spirits? This *is* fairy country."

"Big white angels," Russell said.

"What proof have you?"

Mrs. Russell rose. "We have a plethora of proof," she said, barely opening her eyes. "Enlarged glands. . ."

"Photographs," Russell corrected her.

"Enlarged photographs. Plaster casts of footprints. Large fingerprints which have no swirls or whorls"—she lifted her arm, her big hand spiraling upward.

"And of course we have the best proof of all," Russell said. "The angels themselves."

I spoke: "There are angels *here*?"

"Precisely!" Russell answered.

Servants wheeled in a table bearing a display: a plaster print of a large, five-toed foot with a horn-like projection at the heel—a talon, Russell called it; a dozen photographs, Dr. Horace's work: foggy shots of a figure in white. In one picture the angel was coming headfirst through the wall for what was certain to be a very awkward landing at the foot of the stairs. And there were fingerprints, made by fingers large as sausages.

Russell led us into the hall to the spot where the angel had flown through the wall. "Here," Russell said. "His handprint."

In the post at the foot of the stairs a smooth handprint was sunk two inches into the marble. "Apparently the fellow leaned on it," Koch mumbled.

"Notice the size," Russell said. "Sixteen inches from the base of the hand to the tip of the middle finger."

I stepped forward and put my hand into the impression. When I touched the stone I felt a strange warmth.

In the study again, Russell informed us that last evening he and Mrs. Russell, while strolling in the garden, had met an angel among the rose bushes. "Hello, there," the angel said, and had talked to them for several hours.

Russell went on, but at that point I slipped out the nearest French door. I crossed the terrace and went into the garden.

*

The sky was dusty with stars, and the cold scent of flowers filled the air. A mist lay in the garden and as I walked along the path it was as though I were wading in a pond. I lit a cigar and waited.

Nothing happened.

Naturally. Russell knew how to do a thing. I thumped away the cigar.

But as I was leaving the garden, I felt someone close behind me.

I refused to turn. I went up onto the terrace. Then I felt as if I was being watched—not by the person in the garden, but by others. Perhaps Russell and the rest were watching from the black windows of the house.

I woke shouting and shaking my fist at Russell. I was in bed, and the light of day filled the room. I lay a while in the deep silence of my house.

Then outside the door there was a commotion—people running, shouting.

I dressed quickly and unlocked my door. A young servant came running down the hall at top speed. I grabbed his arm. "Let me go," he said, rolling his eyes.

"What's the trouble?" I yelled in his face.

"Emergency! Mr. Russell!"

Downstairs, servants rushed about. "What is happening?" I called.

"Are you ready for breakfast, sir?" A round-faced maid appeared before me.

"I don't want breakfast, my dear. I want to know what the trouble is."

"The Koch family, sir," the girl said. She was very pretty—round cheeks and clear eyes. "Something awful has happened."

After asking her name—Rose!—I hurried down the corridor to Koch's suite.

It was full of smashed furniture and shattered plaster. A

huge hole was torn in a corner.

In the center of the room Professor Koch was tending to his wife, who was badly battered. Their daughter—naked from the waist up—sat on a pile of debris while Dr. Horace dreamily globbed salve on a bruise in the center of her bony chest.

"What happened?" I asked.

"Big snakes," Dr. Horace said and winked.

Koch turned from his wife. "Giant boa constrictors tore into the house and attacked us," he said. "Thank goodness Russell came when he did. He saved our lives."

At that moment Russell entered from the next room. "Just look," he said, rolling up his shirt sleeves. Large snakebites tracked both arms. They resembled red hoofprints.

"But I killed one," Russell said. "I fought three at once and crushed the head of one. Like this"—he clasped his hands. "Its head burst," he shouted. "Blood squirted out. It was like a fire hose."

"After the attack," Koch said, "the other snakes dragged off the dead one."

"Astounding!" I exclaimed. "How many were there in all?"

"A baker's dozen," Koch's daughter answered, and pushed away Dr. Horace's hand.

Rose was waiting outside. "Come this way, sir," she whispered and took my hand. We tiptoed down the hall.

She sat me at the kitchen table and served breakfast. The servants one by one were sneaking out the back door, carrying their bags. "And what about you, my dear?" I asked Rose.

"I wouldn't leave you, sir." Her eyes were large and deep.

"And what will come of all this?" I asked.

"Mr. Russell won't back down," she said. "That is certain. He will go on and on. Until the worst."

When I left the kitchen I saw Professor Koch's back as he went out the front door. I followed.

At the foot of the steps Koch was waving at the taxi coming down the road. His wife and daughter leaned against each other. Mrs. Koch saw me and came over. "We must leave," she said with animation, her eyes flashing. "The Professor has had second thoughts about this angel business." We looked at the Professor. He stared across the road into the woods. Mrs. Koch stepped closer to me and whispered low, "If I were you, I would give it up. Mr. Russell is insane, but this time he is onto something."

"He is? What?" I asked.

"The Professor believes Mr. Russell has become an angel."

The cab turned up the driveway. The old driver stumbled out and loaded the bags into the trunk. The Kochs got in and drove off without waving, without even looking back.

At dinner Rose served the five of us. We were silent through the meal. Russell sat brooding at the head of the table.

At last Mrs. Russell spoke. "The Kochs left just when matters were becoming clear."

"The Kochs cannot be blamed," Russell said. "Plainly, those snakes were a put-up job. The sort of thing an angel just can't resist."

"The Kochs are cowards."

"My dear Mrs. Russell," Dr. Horace said, slumping so low in his chair he seemed about to slide under the table. "*I'm* a coward and *I* have remained. Let's give credit where credit is due, shall we?"

She ignored this and said to Russell, "Tonight we must try."

He seemed not to hear. Then without looking up, he said, "No. There's too much against it."

"But we've come this far."

"Maybe too far."

"If you refuse, I shall without you," she said.

"Very well. Tonight." He looked across the table at me. "Are you with us?"

"I suppose," I said. "But what exactly is it we're going to do?"

They stared at me—even Rose, standing behind Russell's chair. "Why," Russell said slowly, "we shall . . . *seize* it."

"Oh. Well then—yes. Count me in!"

We were stationed at strategic locations through the house where the angel might appear. My location was on the balcony overlooking the front lawn and the road. I was equipped with a walkie-talkie, and armed with a bow and arrows, as was Russell. It was his theory that angels could be intimidated by these weapons—and these only.

The night was clear and cold under the moon. I faced the silent forest across the road.

It was well past midnight. Now and then a voice cheeped from my walkie-talkie. I leaned against the wall. Wind moved through the forest . . .

The walkie-talkie woke me—not with the piping voice of one of the others, but with an urgent spizz of static.

I spoke into the walkie-talkie. Nothing. I shook it, struck it, but received no reply.

I hurried off the balcony and inside. I ran down the dark corridor, my footsteps echoing.

I stopped, holding my breath and listening.

Black silence. Then laughter—far away.

I hurried from room to room, but didn't find Russell and the others.

I again listened. At first, nothing. Then again the distant laughter. But somewhat louder. Then the voices were gone. I waited in the darkness.

Again I heard them—in the next room!

I rushed down the hall to the dining room. But it was empty. I held my breath. Silence.

I returned to the study . . .

And heard their voices, distinctly now, from the wall separating the study and the dining room.

I approached the wall which was covered with a ceiling-high bookcase. I stood near it. I heard them talking and laughing.

With my face nearly touching the books, I moved down the bookcase. I stopped. I could nearly make out the words the tiny voices spoke.

I took a book from the shelf. In its empty space I saw a room and they were sitting in a circle—Russell, Mrs. Russell, Dr. Horace and Eunice, and Rose!

I started to call to them.

But then Russell lifted both arms and stood. He crossed the circle and stood before Rose.

I wanted to turn away, but couldn't. Though Rose turned her head, she stood and stepped forward.

"Don't," I whispered. "Please don't." She began undressing.

Russell stripped . . . and Professor Koch was correct! Naked, Russell looked like a huge white pigeon.

I replaced the book. I turned to the windows, silver and hard with moonlight.

"Bad luck last night," Russell said the next morning when he came into the dining room where I sat alone. "No angels hereabouts, after all." He reached down and took a strip of bacon from my plate.

Rose came in, carrying a tea pot. When she saw Russell, she looked down and mumbled.

"Speak up, girl," Russell said.

"Would you care for breakfast, sir?"

"No," he said. "Haven't time." Turning to me, he extended his hand. "I hope my stay has been as edifying for you as it has been pleasant for me."

"Indeed," I said and stood.

We walked down the hall to the door. "Mrs. Russell, Dr. Horace and Eunice left early this morning," he said.

"You've done everything," I said.

"Yes. Everything is taken care of," Russell said quite busily.

"But not quite," I said low.

"What's that?"

We stood on the steps. The black taxi waited in the driveway.

"There's the matter of Rose," I said, and he glanced at me.

"Oh." He chuckled. "So you know. Well." His shoulders lifted in a huge shrug. "I hardly know what to say."

"Will you be taking her with you?"

He looked at me with puzzlement and something like disappointment—or offense. "No. Why should I?"

I nodded once and looked away.

"I say," he went on. "I hope this won't come between you and me."

"Only somewhat."

"That's more like it. Time cures, they say." He stepped nearer, again we shook hands, and while he skipped down the steps I turned and reached into the umbrella stand inside the door.

At the cab he turned to wave. I shot. The arrow struck him in the chest. He fell into the back seat of the taxi, which lurched forward, slamming the door. The car drove down the road.

Of course I didn't shoot him—though I had entertained several variations of the scene before Russell came downstairs, said good-bye, got in the taxi, and rode off, waving out the rear window.

When the car disappeared down the road and the sound of its motor died, I went into the house. "Rose," I called. My voice echoed deep into the house.

I went into my study, lit a cigar, and stood at the window. The sky was low and the forest awaited the burials of winter.

I turned to my desk. Soon Rose's sister was by my side—her name was Lily. She lit a cigarette and let it dangle in the corner of her mouth. "I like that," she whispered, and put her hand on my shoulder.

HOUSE-HUNTING NEAR THE FRONTIER

We walked up the steps of the big house. From the porch we could see the city, tiny in the distance.

Father unlocked the front door with the key he had got from the real estate people, and we went in.

The room was vast and empty. There was nothing for us to look at but its largeness and the fireplace. Mother started talking. She immediately understood the house and how she felt about it. The next thing was to make Father feel the same way. While Mother talked to Father we walked through the other rooms on the first floor and came to a large staircase. We started up, and the stairs went on and on. We stopped to catch our breath, turning and looking back at the room far below. We reached the second floor and a wide hall with hundreds of doors. We started down the hall. We walked and walked but it seemed to me we were getting nowhere. Father apparently had the same feeling because he started complaining. But as usual he didn't complain about the right thing. (I never understood that in Father: it was as if he were hiding from himself.) This time he chose to complain about me.

Mother became interested in what he was saying. She agreed with him, though she admitted the particulars Father brought up hadn't occurred to her. But clearly Father had given considerable thought to the matter. Mother pitched in and the two of them complained heartily about me as we went down the endless hallway, with me in the middle. Then we came to another stairs, and fell silent.

The staircase was little wider than a person's hips, and each step was cut shallowly. Climbing these stairs would be like going up a ladder.

Father pointed at the stairs and looked at me. I started climbing. Looking down between my feet I saw Father was following, and Mother was somehow climbing after him.

We went up and up. It seemed we climbed for several hours, and of course we paused several times to rest. I was discouraged and believed we would go on climbing forever—but I told myself I only thought that because I was merely a child and children think such things. Finally we reached the top and, panting, stood looking down a hall.

The floors were ripped up, big hunks were torn from the ceiling and walls, doors were pulled off their hinges and lay scattered among the boards and piles of debris.

Father mumbled to himself, but then he and Mother went on and I hurried to keep up with them.Then as if they had found what they were looking for, we stopped before a door that was still intact. We stared at it as if it were a picture in a museum.

It was a large brown door and the knob was a gnome's head: bulging eyes, big nose, grinning mouth with the tip of its tongue sticking out. The knob was shiny from use, and I wasn't surprised—after all, hadn't we traveled all this way to find it? I felt reassured and was ashamed that when we were climbing the narrow stairs I had thought Mother and Father were making a big mistake.

Then Father reached for the knob. His hand traveled the distance to the knob with such slowness that I had plenty of time to think: I thought about my dog Spot and my cat Urbane who were home waiting for me, and I thought about Mother, how she was probably at this moment also thinking about the door and how slowly Father's hand was moving. I had plenty of time to think even beyond that, and I went clear to the frontiers of utter boredom as the hand moved for the knob.

It reached the knob and began turning it. It turned and turned. We waited. *I* waited. Then Father started opening the door.

Mother and I stepped back to allow plenty of room. Farther back—stumbling over debris. Farther back. With both hands Father forced the door wide open.

There was a perfect closet. Even I recognized it perfection.

Father nodded, turned to me, and with his right hand motioned to the closet.

I felt Mother's hand on my shoulder, not pushing, but communicating as explicitly as if she had touched her big lips to my ear and put the words into me.

I stepped into the closet, turned, and looked out at them standing on a pile of debris, the cracked and ruined wall behind them . . .

After Father shut the door, they stayed out there a long time, talking. Then they walked up and down the hall, stopped outside the closet, and talked again. There was a hush, and I knew Father had put his ear to the closet.

"I'm still in here, Father," I whispered.

They walked off and I knew they went down to the second floor, then down the other stairs to the first floor, then to the huge room where they probably stood looking at the fireplace, and then they went to the front door, waited a moment, thinking about . . . I don't know. Maybe they had a conversation. Then they went out the door and shut it after them.

They have gone farther than our home. They have gone to another country. I am still here and will be, I suppose, until I can do something about this closet, the door, then the hall—all that debris, all the shattered walls and the ripped up floorboards, and then all the rooms on this floor and so on . . . to downstairs. Last of all I'll have to do something about that fireplace. But until I do everything, I wait. I'm not waiting for someone to open the closet door. I would be foolish to be waiting for that—and, after all, I wasn't born yesterday.

*   *   *

THE LOVE OF BEASTS

Sunday evening. The woman in black, the thin young woman in the second pew, is the minister's wife, Maureen. Look! She leans forward as if she will kneel between the pews, though William hasn't yet called for that; later, at the climax of his sermon, he will rear back and command the congregation to humble themselves on the floor of God's house.

Maureen's eyes appear closed tight. Perhaps she is searching for a vision of William and God locked in a holy grapple that will consecrate him, Maureen, and the entire congregation. But let us move nearer.

Her lips are thin and bloodless purple, the lips of an ascetic. Her eyes are open a tiny crack through which she sees an empty gray field. Maureen can rise and walk off into that field . . .

Suddenly the church is quiet. But Maureen doesn't lift her head; William often pauses, letting the congregation appall itself with silence.

A deacon on the front row turns, for William is staring toward the back of the church. Maureen turns, and she is the first to speak, if it can be called that: to the congregation's great amazement and shame, Maureen fills the church with a loud wet sucking sound.

"Praise God," William says again and again. Women are sobbing. The deacon takes another turn embracing Andrew.

"I'm sorry," Andrew says loudly.

"I am thankful," William says for everone to hear. "All of us are thankful. At last my brother has returned. Praise God!"

"I should stayed outside," Andrew says. "Till you got it done."

William raises his voice: "This is God's work."

"Praise God," they murmur.

"Let us kneel," William says. "Let us put our knees on the floor of God's house humbly and offer thanks for the return of this prodigal person." His voice rises—"The prodigal has returned. From evil, the prodigal has returned. From black sin where he walked, the prodigal has returned . . ."

Maureen has knelt but she does not bow her head. She watches Andrew, her eyes wide. He is grinning at her.

The deacon and a handful of others come to the parsonage and sit at the kitchen table drinking coffee while William discusses Andrew's career of sin.

Standing by the stove, Maureen watches Andrew. He wears a green suit several sizes too small, a white shirt, and a blue flowered tie. As William talks, Andrew nods his enormous head, and once he tries to add to William's remarks, but he stammers and stops. He sits holding the edge of the table with both hands, as if he might at any moment push it away or turn it over. His hands are huge. Maureen has never seen such fingers.

His face . . . Maureen is certain that in prison the guards put his head in a machine that squeezed it until it was twice as long as a normal head. His nose is huge, his eyes as big as eggs.

William finishes with Andrew's soul and leans back and yawns.

The deacon rises, reaches across the table and again shakes Andrew's hand. The others take a final turn, say good-night, and leave by the back door.

William and Andrew go into the living room, and Maureen washes the dishes. She smiles at her reflection in the black window over the sink. She stretches her mouth until the smile is a gash, her thin face arrogant, fierce. She balloons her cheeks, then gapes, showing all her teeth, her lips stretched until they hurt. She lolls her tongue and tilts her head, her tongue sliding from one corner of her mouth to the other. Sticking out her tongue as far as it will go, she closes her eyes and slowly licks her lips, around and around . . .

In the living room William says, "God forgives you, Andrew, and so do I, but we haven't forgotten, and we don't want you to ever forget what you did. You've had twelve years to repent for the life you stole from an innocent, unsuspecting person. I hope you prayed constantly those twelve years and looked deep into your heart. Did you?"

Andrew nods his big head.

"Good." The house is silent. William calls to the kitchen—"If you're done with those dishes, come in here."

Maureen enters and Andrew speaks to her: "She looks like the picture."

"What pictures." William says quickly.

Andrew's huge fingers carefully take a snapshot from his billfold. William glances at it—"Huh."—and hands it back.

"It was when you got married," Andrew says.

"Much has happened since then," William says. "To you, nothing has changed since you've been away. Because you're a fool, Andrew, you erroneously believe everything has waited. But *nothing* waited. You have been left behind. And now you come and lay at my feet the responsibility of your life."

Andrew lowers his head.

"To bed." William stands. "There's a cot in the basement. You can sleep there." William takes hold Andrew's elbow and steers him through the kitchen to the basement door. "Goodnight, Andrew. Tomorrow you begin a new life."

Maureen follows William upstairs. In her room as she undresses she feels Andrew listening. She knows he hears her open and shut her closet door and hears the creak of her bedsprings.

*

In Andrews's new life he follows at William's heels like a giant dog. People stare as they walk down the street, and William knows they are laughing. It occurs to him that for some reason God has sent Andrew to punish him, and this sends William into a deep preoccupation. He continues with all his duties; but he is profoundly distracted. He revives now and then, such as the morning when William is "on the air" broadcasting the WHOD "Holy Hour" : he looks up and is alive—free!—for a bright, splendid moment. But then through the big studio window he sees Andrew sitting in the waiting room, his giant hands on his knees.

During the Wednesday night sermon William can barely see the congregation. The light in the church is strangely dim; before him the congregation seems submerged in a yellow pond.

Several days later when Andrew comes up from the basement William is waiting in the kitchen. Maureen is at the stove.

"Andrew, you can't come with me today," William says. "Or tomorrow. Not any more." Then William turns away. He cannot look at Andrew or at Maureen, who has turned. He avoids their eyes as if he were speaking to a Sunday school class of high school boys and girls. He looks at the floor, then the ceiling. "Andrew, the best thing for you is steady employment. I will find something for you."

Andrew stares down at his feet.

"Today," William goes on, "I will keep you in mind as I make my rounds. Jobs are scarce, but with my influence I will find . . ."

Andrew opens his mouth and makes a thick, low gargle which becomes words, "Inside I helped the chaplain. I was his 'sistant."

William nods. "Very commendable."

"I can be your 'sistant. I can do things."

William purses his lips. "Um," he says to the refrigerator.

He rubs his eyes with the tips of his fingers. "All right. For the time being. Today you can sweep out the church and empty the . . . empty the . . ."

"Waste cans," Maureen says.

"Yes." William gestures vaguely, as if he were brushing mosquitoes from his face. Then he turns to Maureen. "Isn't breakfast ready yet?"

Maureen cleans her bare little room and goes downstairs with her dirty bedsheets. As she passes the door to the living room, where Andrew is watching television, she doesn't look in. In the basement she puts the sheets in the washer and switches it on. In the noise under the low ceiling she can't hear him now if he walks from the living room . . .

She goes to his cot. She closes her eyes, leans over it, and takes a deep breath. She yanks up the sheets and stuffs them into the washing machine with the others. She leans against the churning machine.

Upstairs she stands in the kitchen waiting, then she goes to the living room. Andrew sits in William's chair, his hands hanging over the ends of the arm rests. "Do you want a cup of coffee?" Maureen says.

"Sure." He rises from the chair and walks across the room, shaking the floor and the walls, making the tiny china dogs and cats skitter on their knickknack shelves. Maureen turns off the television set. When she enters the kitchen he is sitting at the table and as she puts the coffee pot on the stove she feels him watching her.

He laughs loudly. "I used to think about this all the time." He shakes his big head. "Just this way. You and me would drink a cup of coffee. And here it is." His large eyes are unblinking. "I used to think about you all the time. I dreamed about you. Now here it is."

Maureen is sinking. Her eyes swallow everything into her. She turns to the stove.

She pours the coffee and sits across the table from him. He

noisily drinks his coffee, puts down his cup, and grins. Then he rises and goes into the living room. He switches on the television set, and Maureen hears a boom of voices.

William comes home late that afternoon. He doesn't say hello but squints at Maureen, then goes through the kitchen and looks into the living room. Andrew sits before the television set. "Hello, William," he says.

William goes upstairs and stays in his room until Maureen calls him to supper. He eats fast, his face low over his plate, his bald spot staring at Maureen and Andrew. Maureen picks at her food. The she feels William looking at her. She faces him, and his eyes shift down to his plate.

And Maureen almost cries out, for suddenly she knows that William wants it too.

Knowing takes her breath. Her face burns and she bows her head, unable to look at either of them, burning with shame and glee.

The next morning after breakfast William leaves in the car, and a few minutes later Andrew also leaves the house. Maureen watches him plod down the sidewalk toward town, swinging his arms. She stands at the window until he returns, carrying a paper sack. He goes straight downstairs.

That night William goes to the church for a board meeting and he allows Andrew to come along. Maureen goes to the basement.

Beside the cot is the paper sack, the top folded in a neat cuff, and in it are candy wrappers and cigarette butts which Andrew drowned out either under the faucet or with spit: she pictures him carefully drooling on a large finger and touching it to a cigarette.

A green transistor radio is smudged with chocolate fingerprints: she sees him holding it while he lies on his back . . .

Under the thin mattress are comic books, a pair of little scissors, and men and woman and animals Andrew has cut out. There are also magazines of naked women smiling cruelly. She picks up another magazine, looks at it, and draws her elbows tight to her sides. The magazine is full of naked men standing with their hands on their hips. The magazine slips from her fingers. She lies down on the cot and stares at the cobwebbed floorbeams overhead, her heart pounding hard. She tries to keep from thinking, but in spite of herself she sees the men in the magazine, one of them in particular: a handsome young man wearing a big sombrero grins and aims himself at Maureen.

The days are ponderous with hours, nights are endless as Maureen lies in bed lost to darkness, teeth clenched, eyes wide, afraid of what awaits her in sleep. She glides through the night with her legs apart.

Cooking their breakfast she leans against the stove without seeing the food or smelling it. William watches her constantly. Andrew eats enough for four men, then plods back down the basement stairs like a horse returning to its stable.

William's sermons are thrilling, inspiring, incoherent: words spurt out of control and ababble with damnation, he sees for them all a universe of sin, he analyzes the holy principle of wrath in goodness, and at the top of his lungs he speculates about devastating redemptions.

Head bowed, Maureen listens to William and squinting, she creates a swamp and places William in it wearing his black suit, his face perfectly round, his bald spot shining. In the swamp William preaches to stumps. The sky is a thick intersticing of snake scales.

On the afternoon of that inevitable day, William comes in the back door and stops short as if he has been hit. His nostrils quiver. Sweat pops out all over his face. He *knows*!

At the stove Maureen doesn't turn to greet him. *That* speaks it!

And he can smell it in the house, like wet dogs.

"Is he here?" William says, his voice level though he is turning purple.

Leaning over the stove, Maureen shakes her head.

"Where? At town?"

"I don't know."

"All right," William says. He is panting. "All right. Then I will wait. Yes." He walks across the kitchen and back. "We will eat supper without him. Yes." His hands fly up and he claws his bald spot. "Immediately!" he shouts.

Maureen flies back and forth between the table and the stove. William sits down and rattles off grace, not lowering his head but watching Maureen set the table. She walks stiffly. Her lips are pink and swollen.

She sits down and he can tell that at first it is painful for her to take food into her mouth. But then she eats faster and faster, greedily, chewing with her mouth open, stuffing food in with both hands, and she looks up at William, her nostrils flared, her eyes bright . . . "Stop that!" he shouts.

In the silence they hear laughter below. "Agh," William says. His eyes bulge. He leaps to his feet and bounds across the kitchen and down the basement stairs. "Ah hah!" he yells and Maureen hears scuffling. William roars, then words emerge: ". . . again . . . damnation . . . obey. Listen to me. Damnation."

Splat! Someone is struck. Again—again. Maureen goes to the door and slowly walks down the stairs.

Andrew sits on his cot with his hands folded in his lap. His head jerks to the side when William strikes him.

William turns to Maureen, his fist drawn back. "There," he yells and points to a glint on the floor—a hunting knife. "Look what I found him playing with. And there. A gun."

Maureen can't see it . . . unless the spider shadow by the wall is a gun. Yes. Black and shrewd: a pistol.

"And these." William grabs a handful of magazines and throws them up. One is snagged by a nail in the floorbeams and hangs there. William knocks it fluttering across the basement.

"He will not change," William pants. "Twelve years.

Murder. A man's *life*. For nothing. And the damnation. The eternal damnation!" William reaches down for the hunting knife . . .

Maureen backs toward the stairs. But William is only gathering up the knife and the gun. Holding them in one hand, he bends and picks up the magazines with the other.

William faces Maureen. "And you. *You*." His lips work, his face strains, but no words come. He goes upstairs.

Andrew pulls the sheet off his cot and crosses the basement to the faucet. He wets the sheet and holds it to his face. He returns to the cot and grins at Maureen. His face is swollen as if mushrooms bulge under the skin.

He goes down on his knees and reaches into the crack between two big cardboard boxes. He withdraws his hand and it holds what Maureen thinks at first are black bones. Andrew stands and put his hand into the thing.

At the top is a hatchet; the other end of the short handle is a dagger. Set in the knuckle-guard are steel burrs. Andrew grins and chops air.

Maureen lies in the night waiting for sleep and death, but she knows she will never sleep again. But when the door opens she has been asleep, or in that dawn-quiet state between waking and the pandemonium of dreams. The shadow in the door isn't Andrew but William. He hesitates, his head turns back and forth—the room is unfamiliar—and he shuts the door behind him. The room is dark but she sees him, a shadow, moving toward the bed. "What do you want?" she says distinctly but not loudly.

He stops. "I . . ." She hears him opening and shutting his mouth. "You're my wife and . . ."

"I don't care. I don't want you in here," she says louder. "This is my room."

She feels the nudge as he bumps the bed—she has guided him with her voice—and she moves toward the wall.

He talks louder, speaking swiftly and to Maureen's

amazement in the dark William sounds like a young man. But his *words* reach her. She tries to ignore what he is saying, but with the determination of insects the words penetrate the dark.

She listens coldly. His voice now strangely boyish, William informs her they have been man and wife four years but there has never been love in their marriage. He had hoped she would find in herself the humility and holy resignation of love; but that not until this miraculous transformation, which William explains is true love, could they truly be married, and now she has demonstrated that she will never be capable of sublime abnegation. She has proven she is capable only of base love, arrogant, prideful, the love of beasts.

So Maureen must go away. William will tell the church board that he woke one morning and she had vanished.

"Above all, I cannot abide what you have done to my brother," William says, still louder. "You will leave and I will guide him. If there can ever be hope in this pitiful existence, it can only come through my love. Tommorrow when you are gone he will come up to this room and sleep in this bed.

"Do you see how thoroughly you are rejected? Do you now see that you are evil and that I am casting you out? I could spend my entire life laboring for your salvation, but all my efforts would be for nothing. And meanwhile Andrew would sink into deeper ruination, for I cannot reach him with you in this house. You are a barrier between Andrew and me, and because he is simple and weak, you are stealing him away. I see it clearly.

"God has spoken to me, and His Word is clear. Though it means your ruin and the loss of your immortal soul, I must *cast* you out. Now all I can do for you, Maureen, is pray that someday you will open your heart and accept God's mercy on you and let Him *raise* you from your evilness. Oh, let us pray."

Maureen moves across the bed to kneel on the floor beside him. She reaches the edge and putting her feet down discovers she has put her legs against William. Her gown has ridden up her thighs, and as Andrew glides into the room he sees

William's head between Maureen's knees.

Maureen sits before the television set. The picture is on, the sound is off. Habits twit at the back of her mind: she could make coffee or clean the house, yes, she must clean the house, the mop and a bucket of water, first upstairs in her room, then the hall, the stairs, through the kitchen, the basement stairs . . .

The night is silent. Trembling, she stares at the television screen.

Andrew comes into the room. He has slicked down his hair and wears his green suit, shirt, and blue flowered tie. He walks across the room and picks up the telephone. "I want to go to St. Louis," he says into the receiver. "St. Louis," he says louder. "I don't have a number any more." He listens. "He is Robber Robber." Andrew turns to Maureen and says loudly, "Tell her." Maureen stares straight ahead. "His name," Andrew says. "*His* name. Robert . . ." into the phone—"*Robert.*" He waits, listening. "Robert two times. Robber Robber."

Maureen watches the television screen. The night won't end. All the lights in the house burn but the room is dim and there are no windows or doors in the house and the house is filled with the smell of meat.

"Here." Andrew pulls her from the chair and across the room.

"What's he done this time?"—a man's voice in the phone.

"William?" Maureen says.

"Who is this?" the voice says. "Where's Andy?"

Maureen looks at Andrew's swollen face. His eyes are huge. He is nodding at her.

Maureen tells the voice in the phone the name of the town and the address of the parsonage.

*

It is day when Maureen opens her eyes. A man is talking to Andrew. He is as tall as Andrew and wears a gray sweater and a hood pulled over his head and drawn tight with a string, squeezing his face into a fist. "Okay. Her too." He looks at Maureen. "What's wrong with her?"

They lift her from the chair. "Christ," the man says. The seat of the chair is soaked.

Andrew brings clothes into the room and they dress her. Then they take her outside and put her in the back seat of a car. She wakes in a hotel room where brown men balloon from stains on the walls and ceiling. Andrew stands by the window cutting pictures from comic books.

Three cabins squat at the end of the dirt road. A wooden sign nailed to a fence post says ***Lake Vu***. A mud-splattered car with its hood raised is parked in front of the center cabin, and an incredibly thin man, made of sticks, is working on the car. "There's Mr. Goforth," Robert says. The man walks over to their car and looks into the back seat at Maureen. His face is a gray, sharp triangle. "Well, well," Mr.Goforth says and laughs quickly.

They get out and go with him into the center cabin. There is a bed, a chair, and a sink with the faucets broken off.

Robert hands him some money and Mr. Goforth counts it. "Nice friend you got," Mr. Goforth tells Andrew. Andrew is wearing his suit and shirt and tie. His shirt is sweat-soaked and his suit is speckled with foodstains. Andrew stares at Mr. Goforth.

"You watch out for them, okay?" Robert says.

"Sure," Mr. Goforth says. "I'll come and watch. Ain't that right?" he asks Andrew. "That's real good citement."

Robert leaves and Mr. Goforth goes back out and works on his car. Andrew sits in the chair and starts cutting out a comic book. Maureen lies on the bed and mosquitoes hang in the air above her.

The hood of the car slams and Mr. Goforth comes into the cabin with a short three-legged stool. He picks up one of Andrew's cut-outs, a little man with a gun in his hand, and turning to Maureen, Mr. Goforth solemnly dances the little man in the air.

He sits on his stool and looks first at Andrew, then at Maureen. "You know what, Andy?" Andrew is busy. "I like a pretty face." His smile is a crooked line in his face. "Is she real good to you, Andy?"

The cabin is silent.

Looking over his shoulder at Andrew, Mr. Goforth rises from the stool and moves to the side of the bed. "I love you," he whispers. His hand hovers over her face. A mosquito lands on the thumb. "Andy, I want to touch her."

He touches her cheek. She closes her eyes and he touches her eyelids. "You are beautiful," he whispers. He touches her lips and works a finger into her mouth. Leaning over the bed, he runs his hand up between her legs. He stops when she moans.

He goes out to his car and comes back with two pistols. "Here." Andrew holds them and grins.

Mr. Goforth speaks loudly: "When they get here, you tell them you got a message from Lead City, huh? Give me them things." Mr. Goforth goes to the door, cocks the pistols' hammers, and fires them. The gunfire shakes the cabin. In the ringing silence that follows, Mr. Goforth hands the guns to Andrew. "They'll think you're a cowboy."

Mr. Goforth goes out the door and Maureen hears the car's starter grinding. Then the car starts and Mr. Goforth races the motor and it backfires. Andrew stands in the doorway, laughing and waving the pistols.

Mr. Goforth drives off and the sound of the motor hangs in the air as the car goes down the road.

*

Andrew walks around the room pointing the pistols, dodging, bending his knees, shaking the guns—"*Daah! Daah!*"—at the empty doorway. Then they hear the car.

Andrew steps out the door as the car comes nearer, and Maureen knows it is going to happen now, the car louder . . . It stops. A door slams. Then she hears Mr. Goforth.

He and Andrew come into the cabin. "Come on," Mr. Goforth tells her, and Maureen feels herself moving off the bed but she can't walk. He takes her arm and they walk outside. She squints in the sunlight.

Andrew is standing by the car, the guns in his hands, his long face watching Maureen and Mr. Goforth. "She is supposed to go with me," Mr. Goforth says. Andrew's mouth opens, but the sound is not words but a broken sigh, like a man humming in his sleep. "Just ask Robert Robert," Mr. Goforth says and opens the car door. He shoves Maureen in and slams the door. He goes around, gets in the other side, and starts the motor. He races the motor and they take off.

Maureen sees the trees on both sides of the road, and beyond the trees, empty fields. Faster, the trees blur by as the car bounces down the dirt road, and they top a hill and start down the other side. "Made it!" Mr. Goforth yells. "Hot damn!" He pounds the steering wheel. "What *do* you think of that?"

"Fine," Maureen says, hearing her voice and knowing for a moment that she is still inside this flesh, seeing large green trees, a sky.

WITH THE MORY BOT

We were on our porches waiting for the rain, when some boys ran through the village shouting that strangers were coming up the river. We went down to the landing and saw a boat with six oarsmen and, standing in the bow, a tall man clutching a book to his chest. At the other end sat a slender woman in a long white dress and a hat with a veil. As the boat drew to shore she lifted the veil and smiled stiffly at a point beyond us. The man spoke, not to the woman or the oarsmen, but either to himself or to us; we strained to hear what he was telling us.

"You have forgotten your duty," Reverend Treet said and shook his large head. We had finished lunch and Reverend Treet, his wife Felicity, and I sat on my porch.

"But so far my only duty here has been to tinker with the tower," I said.

"Hasn't it occurred to you there is more than that?"

Felicity Treet laid her cold hand on mine. "There is more for all of us," she whispered. "We must spread love."

I bowed my head. "I guess I forgot." Felicity withdrew her hand and, leaning back, looked beyond me.

"You haven't forgotten your teachings, have you?" Reverend Treet said.

"Not exactly."

"You haven't . . . gone over to their ways?"

"Well, yes and no. The fact is, I don't know what their ways are."

The reverend shook his head and spoke to Felicity: "He won't be much help." She seemed not to hear. "Aren't you ashamed of yourself?" he said loudly to me. "You've utterly regressed."

"I'm sorry." Tears rolled down my cheeks.

"I had hoped we could count on you. But you're no better than they."

I sobbed, my shoulders shook.

"I feel he can be trusted," Felicity said.

Reverend Treet put both big hands on the table, leaned on them, and rose to his feet. "The matter is settled. When our supplies catch up we're on to Ran Pangle. While we're waiting . . . stop that sniveling!" I stopped. "While we're waiting, I want you to tell me all you know about them."

"We would tell you everything there is to know about them, but I've never heard of the Ran Pangle."

He frowned down at me. "You're telling the truth?"

"Yes."

"At any rate, we're off for Ran Pangle. I will need some carriers, guides, scouts. You will be my agent—take care of the arrangements." He clasped his hands behind him and paced up and down the porch. "Anything else?" He glanced at Felicity, who sat with her eyes closed. The reverend turned to me. "You mentioned a tower. Do they use it in their rituals? I want to see it."

They followed me through the village and out the path to the tower.

"My word!" Reverend Treet said. "Radar! Does it still function?"

I shrugged. "Once a plane flew over and signaled me to change it two degrees. It hasn't been back."

We returned to the village and I stopped at one of the houses. "Myron," I called, but he wasn't home. "He has gone into seclusion," I told Reverend Treet and Felicity. "The

Myron is our doctor, and my closest friend. He's everyone's closest friend, in fact. He was down at the river when you arrived—he's the one who dyes himself bright blue, with the red forehead."

"Why is he hiding?"

"He's probably worried because you're here. But even when he isn't worried he spends a lot of time with the Other People." I pointed to the high branches above and the small gray-pink monkeys. As ever, a dozen or so were watching us.

Felicity groaned.

"My word!' Reverend Treet whispered. "It's positively eerie."

"I don't see Myron," I said.

"You say he's their leader. Hmm. After I finish with the Ran Pangle I'll spend some time here. Shouldn't take long, these Mory Bot seem a rather passive lot. What's their worship like?"

"We don't really go in for it."

"There's no form of worship?"

"Not exactly. We make special words. Turn things backwards. And we like to tell stories. Some of them are religious, maybe."

"You mean you don't know?"

"None of us are sure, not even Myron. Many of the stories are about animals and night . . ."

"Fear of darkness. Typical."

"No, we're keen on darkness."

"It's all the same. They're heathen—I daresay you agree on that."

He was unaware that as we talked the Other People had started chattering and moving through the branches. It was a great commotion and for me at least very distracting. Glancing up, I saw that now there were hundreds of Other People and clearly they were scolding us. Some shook their small red fists at me.

I looked back at Reverend Treet. "Quite right. We're heathen all the way."

A few days later Reverend Treet's suplies arrived: bibles, horse meat, and tennis shoes. "Enlist some carriers. These supplies must reach the Ran Pangle."

"Yes, sir."

"And you, acting as my agent and translator, will come along."

"I don't know the way."

"Sure you do. You've just forgotten. I think ten carriers should do very well. Are there ten we can trust?"

"Yes."

"Excellent." He pounded me on the back. "Tomorrow we're off!"

"Will Madam be coming?"

He blinked. "Of course not. The Ran Pangle are a nasty bunch. The very worst sort. Felicity will remain here and set to work with the Mory Bot."

I nodded slowly. "She would not be safe with us among the Ran Pangle, but she would be safe alone with the Mory Bot."

He cocked an eyebrow. "She would, rather. Wouldn't she?"

I shrugged and turned away. "I'll try to find ten men I can trust."

"Wait! About this Felicity business. One of us shall remain here. But—" he stroked his chin, "this presents a problem . . ."

"I will take the bibles and horse meat and tennis shoes to the Ran Pangle!" I said. "I will talk to them!"

"You will, eh? And I suppose you'll tell them a story or two." I started to speak. "Silence! You will remain here with Felicity." He put his large hand on my shoulder. "I leave with you a grave responsibility, my good man."

"I shall do my best."

"Excellent. I know you to be a man of your word. Now I must go tell Felicity," and he strode off, wiping his hand on his trousers.

The following morning we waved goodby to the reverend and his band of trusty carriers. Felicity then set to work imparting to the Mory Bot the Boy Lessons, as I translated her teachings about the Christ Child. The tribe hunkered in a circle around Felicity and me. Sitting in her campchair, her legs crossed, Felicity talked for hours, gesturing vaguely with her hands.

That evening after dinner I cleared the table, poured Felicity another cup of coffee, and, backing off, squatted down to wait. She turned to me. "Please come here." I stood across the table from her. "Tell me, are you satisfied with what lies ahead?"

"Not after today," I said. "Not after learning that I am a wretched sinner."

She looked away a moment, then nodded. "I am glad you realize that. But my question was directed less to that point, than to . . ."—she looked from side to side—"this. Have you completely forgotten what you left behind?"

"Yes and no," I said.

"Perhaps you would be interested in some news from home." I smiled. "Well," she said, "would you?"

"Oh yes," I said. "Yes indeed"—and she began.

As she spoke night settled and the yellow rings of the lantern's light drew tighter around the table.

She rapped her spoon on the edge of the table, waking me. "I am afraid I have bored you." Her expression was rigid, her eyes set, her lips a straight line. "Perhaps it would be better if we talked openly. Shall we? You may start." She waited. "Perhaps you would like to tell one of the local parables." She waited. "You may begin."

I took a deep breath and started telling her the story of the old monkey who had fifty wives. It wasn't one of my favorites, but I thought it might interest her. As I spoke I felt night creeping in through my ears. I shook my head and stood straight, breathing deeply, but a shadow glided by the table: a panther, cutting through the village, glanced at me over its shoulder, its large yellow eyes calm and certain. I closed my eyes and kept talking. With the old monkey and his wives we knelt beside a black stream, listening. "Felicity," I whispered and opened my eyes, and I believed she repeated the Mory Bot, the pained stiffness of her face dissolving into the dazzle of the sun on water. With the gaze of dread and glee which we call *flizz*, she leaned down into the reflection of her face in the water, tipping herself dangerously forward.

A week later we had taken our places for the Boy Lessons when we heard shouting down by the river. We hurried to the landing and saw a boat, its rear-half covered with a canopy, coming down the river. Reverend Treet stood in the bow, waving his hands over his head and shouting. Then he ran ahead of the boat!

With his arms out from his sides he ran out onto the water, stood a moment with one foot in front of the other, then turned and dashed back onto the boat.

"Did he actually do that?" Felicity exclaimed.

"He certainly did," I said. The Mory Bot cheered as Reverend Treet performed the feat a second time.

The boat pulled to shore and from under the canopy crawled four giants. Their hair was twisted in big fists bristling with what I hoped were the bones of apes, and clusters of darts which I knew, if they nicked the men's scalps, would turn their brains to copper. These strangers were tattooed with elaborate networks of white curliques; they seemed covered with white lace. Their chief, however, the last to emerge from under the canopy, was reticulated blue, green, and purple. This man, taller even than Reverend Treet and immensely muscular, with a dense and baleful dignity, was sublimely reptilian. His crown was the skull of an anaconda.

Reverend Treet rushed forward, talking rapidly and incomprehensibly. Felicity somehow understood what he was saying and answered in much the same tongue; perhaps it was a religious code, for here and there I heard "temptation" and "grace."

Then Reverend Treet shouted in Felicity's face—"Immediately! He is there among the Ran Pangle." Felicity started to speak but Reverend Treet bellowed, "Listen!"

Towering over us, his face twitching, his eyes big as crocodile eggs, he stared into the jungle. In the silence the chief of the Ran Pangle moved like a smooth ripple behind the reverend, moving closer until he stood pressed against him.

The reverend nodded. "Time has come! We must go up to meet Him. You too"—he grabbed my arm—"and the rest of you"—waving at the Mory Bot who listened with bright eyes, waiting for the funny part.

Reverend Treet went off to the boats, the chief following in lock step.

Felicity smiled vaguely. "He has looked forward to this all his life," she said.

"We're all very happy for him," I said.

"Oh yes," she said softly. "It's even more than he expected."

Reverend Treet led the way in the boat with the Ran Pangle, frequently running out onto the water, though this no longer astonished us: the Mory Bot and I had examined the boat and discovered a narrow prow extending a few inches beneath the water's surface. I assumed the Ran Pangle used this prow in their rituals of tribute to the great snake.

Felicity rode ahead also, and I was in the second boat with Myron, our doctor, who, bright blue from a fresh dyeing, with his forehead a blazing red, appeared from behind a huge ear-shaped frond as we were pushing off. He hopped into my boat and we embraced. "I wish you had come sooner to meet Reverend Treet and Felicity," I told my old friend.

He shrugged his bony blue shoulders. "I know them."

"You do?"

"I've seen it all." His twinkling eyes shot up at the branches sliding by overhead. He had, of course, been up there with the Other People.

"What do you think of the Treets?" I asked.

"Madam Treet has fine moments, but the reverend is dangerous to himself and those around him. He's what I call a fanatic (*razzy-zazza*). But he's nearly done for, now."

"What do you mean?"

"The Ran Pangle," Myron said. "They are going to . . . have him."

"If this is true, we must do something."

Myron shrugged. "There is no way out for Treet. But when the Ran Pangle finish with him they'll be numb—and we'll pick up our things and go home."

"Won't they come after us?"

"They'll forget we were even there."

"Will Reverend Treet . . . suffice?"

"I think he should." Myron leaned back, a sprig of grass in his teeth. "They're not a large tribe. There're just the four of them, not counting their woman."

"There's only one?"

"Right. They . . ."

I clapped my hands over my ears.

I went to Felicity that night as soon as we camped—we would reach Ran Pangle the next morning. "Great danger lies ahead," I told her.

She smiled beyond me.

"You don't understand," I said. "There are . . . terrible things."

"Yes," she said and patted my hand.

I went back to Myron. "What should I do?"

"Do you want her?" Myron said.

"Who?"

"Felicity."

"Oh." I looked away. "I hadn't thought of that, actually." Then I saw it all very clearly. "Yes!"

"Then let Reverend Treet have his way."

"But, after all, we are civilized."

"Quite right. And not only are we civilized, but some of us are gods."

"We are?"

"The Ran Pangle are river gods. Not big ones like the anaconda, but they are gods. And Reverend Treet has dreamed of anacondas for so long . . ."

"He has?"

"Obviously, though of course he would never admit it. But he's in for these Ran Pangle, all the way."

"But even if they're gods, we shouldn't let them . . ." I couldn't say it. "We must warn him," I said.

Myron shrugged. "For form's sake."

We went through the camp to where Reverend Treet and the chief were bedded down. Their eyes blazing in the light of the campfire, they lay like spoons, the chief behind with his arms around Reverend Treet and a leg thrown across him.

"What about the chief?" I whispered to Myron.

"He won't mind."

"But he might jump the gun."

Myron shook his head. "They'll wait till they get home. Here, it wouldn't be the same."

Myron and I squatted down before them.

"Hello," Reverend Treet squeaked.

"The chief is crushing him!" I tried to pull loose the huge arms.

"No!" Reverend Treet said. "This is just fine."

"To the point," Myron said, and I translated. "The chief is going to eat you."

Reverend Treet blinked.

"Ask him," Myron said, touching the nose of the chief

whose chin, hooked over Reverend Treet's shoulder, put their faces cheek to cheek.

"After eating you," Myron went on, "they'll eat the rest of us, one by one."

"What about Felicity?" I said.

"They'll save her for last," Myron said. "They might even skip her and make her queen.It depends on how they feel after they've had us."

"Were you aware of their plans?" I asked Reverend Treet.

He didn't answer, but his eyes sparkled.

"Reverend Treet," Myron said, "believe me, though they are gods, you shouldn't let them do it." He leaned forward and put his face close to theirs. "We can slip off after they fall asleep. By morning they'll forget we were here."

"I can't let them down," Reverend Treet said. "It is love."

Myron nodded and grinned. "*Blorg*," he said—"Ghastly."

"You can't possibly understand," Reverend Treet said. "I've confronted Evil, tracked it to its lair, and . . ." the chief tightened his grip, "I shall triumph," Reverend Treet piped.

Myron glanced at me. "Another Boy Lesson." To Reverend Treet: "You're set on it?"

Reverend Treet nodded as best he could, nodding the chief's head as well.

Our departure from Ran Pangle was as easy as winking at a toad, as we say. On our glide downriver I sat facing Felicity in the boat, watching her cry. "He was a good man," she said.

"Yes," I said.

She put her handkerchief to her face. "The poor savages. We shouldn't leave them up there alone with that awful ignorance."

"They are content," I said. "In their way they are immensely content."

She stared across the smooth water. "You said he was . . . seized by an anaconda?"

I nodded, not looking at her.

"It's amazing. Two months ago the reverend and I were in the rectory on Sudshead Hill. On nice days we had tea in the garden. And now an anaconda . . ." She sighed.

"But," I risked, "in a way he has triumphed."

"Yes—completely. I'm sure that at the crucial moment he felt the . . . majesty." She leaned back and stared at the sky.

When we reached the Mory Bot we helped Felicity to my home, and that night two old women and myself squatted beside the mat where she lay weeping. On the front porch Myron mumbled and chanted all night. He stopped at the first gray of dawn, and I sent the old women away. When they left the room, Felicity reached out. I took her hand and she drew me down to her. "A big snake ate him," she whispered in my ear and giggled. Then she cried with racking heaves and when she stopped she lay panting. The dawn was cool, silent. She turned on her side to me, her eyes hidden in shadow. "Tomorrow I will resume the Boy Lessons"—I'm sure she didn't realize she called them that. "I must continue his work. You will assist me."

"Of course."

"Tell me. No—don't. We will begin lessons for the little children . . . divide them into little groups . . . You must tell me."

"It swam right up and got him."

"He wasn't in long, was he? In spite of being able to walk on water, he was terribly afraid of it."

"The snake came right along. It was simple."

"You mean quick. It was over quickly," she said.

"Yes. A matter of seconds."

"You are so smooth. Your stomach is as smooth as mine. I can't stop crying, even though I know it's what he wanted. Everything comes through me."

I told her the story of the man who lived with birds, giving it Myron's interpretation. Then I told her my favorite—how the trees and animals came, a long story, and by the time I finished she was asleep in my arms. When she woke, at dusk, I was still holding her and she didn't cry. "Go on," she said. I told her about the two feuding families of Other People—again, a long story that could go on forever. We woke at dawn, listening through that gray silence when all things are waiting. She whispered, "What is your name?" I told her, speaking it softly on the dawn: Mory Bot, which means person-who-hurries-home.

MR. SPOON'S VISIT

Such a brilliant morning! Mrs. Dutt had Newfield carry the glass table and three chairs into the garden, and when Mrs. Kilfoil came, the ladies strolled arm in arm along the paths, pausing at each new "yellow pearl," Mrs. Dutt's miniature roses. Then the ladies followed the path into the little maze of japonica, profuse with red blossoms, where they were lost for a delightful moment.

"I so wish I could have been here when your nephew arrived," Mrs. Kilfoil said. "I can hardly wait to meet him."

"He actually arrived twice," Mrs. Dutt said.

"Gracious! How does one manage that?"

"He came in the afternoon, but then he left again."

"You don't mean it!"

"He left his luggage and didn't come home until all hours."

"All hours! Did he explain himself?" Mrs. Kilfoil said.

"Not at all. But he *is* just a boy. I was surprised at what a boy he really is. So . . . incomplete. But he is quite charming in his way. He's very quiet and . . ." Mrs. Dutt's thin lips lifted at the corners in a rather sly smile, "I have the feeling he would like to be unusual."

"How interesting!" Mrs. Kilfoil said.

They turned up the path and returned to the table. Newfield appeared and served coffee.

"Yes, my nephew is charming in his way. And he certainly delights in spending Sister's money!" Mrs. Dutt's laughter tinkled in the still air of the garden. "There has been a parade of deliverymen this morning. Apparently last night he went shopping. They've brought a phonograph, and a peculiar chaise longue, and dozens of pillows, and an extraordinary carpet . . ."

"Where is he putting it all?" Mrs. Kilfoil said. "He is in that lovely large room upstairs, isn't he?"

"He refused to step a foot inside it. So I showed him around and he chose to plant himself in the garden."

Mrs. Kilfoil sat straight. "You mean he's . . . there?" She turned to the little guest house, not forty feet down a path.

Mrs. Dutt nodded.

The doorbell chimed in the distance, and Mrs. Dutt's eyes sparkled. "More of the merry merchants."

"I believe you're enjoying this immensely," Mrs. Kilfoil laughed.

"Perhaps," Mrs. Dutt said, smiling slyly.

But the person whom Newfield showed to the garden was not a deliveryman. He was a well-dressed gentleman, tall and dignified, with silver at his temples and the extravagantly suave, rather strained visage of a sensitive, decently intelligent soul. "Mrs. Dutt?" he said.

"I am she."

"R.C. Spoon." He bowed. "I have come to see your nephew." He approached the table, totally at ease and conveying the impression that he somehow wasn't aware that he had numbed the ladies.

Mrs. Dutt regained speech. "Is it about? . . ." She lifted her hands and twirled two vague circles. "I suppose he's buying more things. Very well." She turned toward the guest house. "He's . . ."

"Ladies." He spoke softly and looked quite directly first at Mrs. Dutt, then Mrs. Kilfoil. "You have here a lovely spot." He glanced about the garden, his gaze pausing on the guest house for just a moment. "Idyllic," he said. "A place of dreams."

"Please, Mr. Spoon," Mrs. Dutt said.

"Thank you. For just a moment," and he sat down. He tilted his head, took a deep breath, and sighed. "Time," he said with his eyes closed. Then he opened them and looked rather sternly at the ladies. In a clear tenor, Mr. Spoon sang:

> The whippets of joy bound down golden ways,
> While harvester Time collects hours and days.

The ladies murmured.

"Thank you," he said, and his brow tightened with two smooth grooves, giving his face an elegant pensiveness. "We hurry along and it is only in rare moments such as this," his hand moved over the garden, "that we realize time has . . . taken us. And that it has taken us with cruel indifference."

"So true!" Mrs. Kilfoil said low.

"I've often thought, that before it's too late I would face up to time and . . ." again the hand moved through the air as if blessing the garden, "stop. For we can, you know. We can stop, really. And then . . ." He reached across, picked up Mrs. Dutt's cup, and took a sip. "Truly taste life."

"Oh! Please!" Mrs. Dutt sputtered. "Won't you please have? . . ."

"Mrs. Dutt," his tone was hushed, urgent, "we so ruthlessly dedicate ourselves to limits, we can't taste life." He closed his eyes and took a deep breath. He whispered, "We can't breathe."

They sat in silence, the ladies large-eyed, their lips parted, watching Mr. Spoon stare afar. He stood and handed Mrs. Dutt a card. He bowed, turned, and walked down the path. He knocked at the narrow door of the guest house and the ladies heard a word from inside. Mr. Spoon answered, the door opened, and he went in.

"What does it say?" Mrs. Kilfoil whispered.

" 'R. Cumington Spoon, Classic Autos.' "

"Do you suppose your nephew is buying a classic auto?"

From the guest house came a burst of harsh laughter. Then a peculiar, metallic grating. The ladies turned toward the little house. "What *was* that?" Mrs. Dutt whispered. Before Mrs. Kilfoil could answer, there was a loud bump inside, and rubbery thrumming sounds rather like bouncing.

"Gracious!" Mrs. Kilfoil said.

The garden was silent a full, tense minute. Then there was a prolonged dragging, scraping—and a truly tremendous crash with the shattering of glass.

"What is happening?" Mrs. Dutt exclaimed.

"Things are breaking," Mrs. Kilfoil said.

"This is awful!" Mrs. Dutt stood, hesitated, glancing at Mrs. Kilfoil. But Mrs. Kilfoil didn't rise from her chair.

Mrs. Dutt marched down the path. As she reached the guest house she heard a furious scuffling and knocking about, with grunting and gasping. Something banged against the wall, rattling the door. Mrs. Dutt rapped on the door and there was abrupt silence inside.

"Yes?" said an odd, tight voice which did not sound like either Mrs. Dutt's nephew or Mr. Spoon.

"Is everything all right in there?" Mrs. Dutt said.

"Yes, thank you."

She waited a moment, but there was no more forthcoming. "Well, I must say . . ."

The phonograph came on with loud, jumpy music that pushed Mrs. Dutt from the door.

She hurried up the path. Mrs. Kilfoil, chalk-white, was standing by her chair. "I really must be going."

"No," Mrs. Dutt said loudly, over the music. "You can't leave now."

The music covered some noise, but the ladies heard more knocking about, and the ultimate—a shuddering crash that fairly shook the guest house and jolted the phonograph needle off the record with a squawk.

The silence was unbearable. But gradually the garden uttered its mild whisper of leaves, and there was the pre-occupied twit of birds. The ladies sat at the table staring rigidly ahead.

The guest house door opened and Mr. Spoon stepped out. Head down, he walked up the path and for a moment it seemed he would pass right by. But he stopped and, turning, revealed his face: it was quite pink, like a child's after a good scrubbing. "Would you ladies accept my invitation to join the Club of Secret Treasures?" he said softly, almost as though offering his condolences. "It really is a nice club; Mrs. Spoon and I are members. The Club is very select and one hundred per cent sincere." He stood straight and sang his radiant tenor:

The mourning dove her love laments,
Yearning for sweet recompense.

"Buffs, hobble-dodgers, and maybe a flam or two, we enthusiastically welcome new members." He bowed, then still bent rushed forward and reached out as if to seize Mrs. Dutt's nose.

From her hair he plucked what at first seemed a red ball. But when he rolled it across the glass table, it untumbled into a bright red rat with a quivery nose and keen little eyes. The ladies gasped. Mr. Spoon reached into Mrs. Kilfoil's hair and out popped a sky blue frog. On the table the rat and the frog looked at the ladies. Mr. Spoon aimed his arm, long and straight, at the rat and frog, and a green snake shot forth. The rat and frog leaped from the table, and the snake slithered off after them and disappeared into the garden.

Mrs. Dutt blinked. "My word!"

"Unexactly earthshaking," Mr. Spoon said, "but fun, you see, and definitely dignified." He licked his lips and straightened his tie. "So give it a think, dear Mrs. Dutt, and call when you decide to join." He bowed. "Good-day." And he was gone.

Mrs. Dutt and Mrs. Kilfoil sat holding their breath. Then a bird swooped from the sky and darted through the garden.

They stood at once and hurried off when they saw the narrow door of the guest house opening.

A VERY MODERN HOME

Helen Droosman's daughter came home to have her baby and get her divorce. Naturally she brought her three little girls with her, Helen's precious granddaughters, rubber stamps of their mother. Two days later Helen had her stroke.

In the hospital Helen woke each morning believing she was in an empty house—for thirty years she had sold real estate. There were other obscurities. Time swiftly padded down the corridor in rubber-soled shoes, or the hours hung motionless like forgotten coats in a closet. Thought was tattered. Words flew through her mind like windblown scraps of paper playing chase in a house where all the windows were broken out. All this was to be expected, Helen was told. She wasn't worried, though she told herself—speaking out loud, which seemed to help—she told herself she *should* be worried. As she lay trying to think this through, ideas stumbled from each others' grasp and lurched down the corridor. What bothered her most was the irregularity of her memory—a radio in another room, sometimes blaring, sometimes so faint she barely heard it over the roar of silence.

But then Helen improved. One day at noon while she was eating a bowl of jello, a giant's huge fingers snapped, sending a shockwave through her, and she was once again herself. "It's over now," she told her daughter Evie who came to visit that evening. "Everything's perfect now, Evie. Isn't that wonderful?"

The next morning Helen announced to her doctor: "I'll live now, Doctor Nye." She laughed loudly, convincingly. The doctor, standing by her bed, patted her foot, smiled, and looked away. "Sure. You'll live a long time."

Helen convalesced at home for a month and then, against Dr. Nye's advice, returned to work. She had no choice—she had been on her own since the death of her husband Rudolph ten years ago. And now Evie had come to stay. Evie was busy being mother to those lovely little girls—she certainly couldn't go out and look for a job. And in her seventh month and her nerves completely shattered by the divorce . . .

So Helen picked up where she had left off. Except her pace was slow, so slow Dr. Nye had nothing to worry about. She worked for a straight salary—she didn't drive herself for those commissions. She was at the real estate office each morning at nine, answered the phone, made all the sales meetings, and showed houses when no other agents were on hand.

And she promised herself she would never again go near the modern house on Twenty-eighth Street. She had been showing it when she had her stroke. A peculiar house, it had stood empty for several years waiting for a buyer. In Helen's slow, echoing dreams in the hospital, the house was a maze in which she searched for faces she had known years ago, following wisps of conversation that passed through the rooms like drafts of cold air.

Then almost by accident Helen made a sale. And another—that not by accident. She was back into it, and in two weeks had regained all the weight Dr. Nye made her lose, but she told herself it wasn't very noticeable, especially with Evie so big, into her eighth month . . .

She did all the running around and endless telephoning necessary in closing the sales, and she was back to normal, she told herself, though she made silly mistakes which she tried to ignore, and though some days passed with an eerie slowness, and perhaps because of their slowness she was very forgetful on those days. Other times it took her by surprise: suddenly everything slid from her mind as if water were pouring over her head. But she was herself again, she insisted. Everything was fine.

Late one afternoon a couple came into the office. They were interested in seeing the unusual modern house advertised in the newspaper.

Helen happened to be the only agent in the office. And the commission on that sale would be a whopper. But thinking of the house gave Helen a queasy, sinking sensation, as if the office were slowly sliding downhill.

"One moment, please," she told the couple and went into the next cubicle. She picked up the phone to call another agent, Hank, home sick with a spring cold. Hank would have risen from his death bed to show that house. Helen's hand, reaching for the dial on the phone, hesitated. She stared at the fat little hand, the short, blunt fingers.

She put down the phone and went into her office. "I'll show the house," she said, smiling at the room.

She added, unable to stop herself, "But we'll have to wait until tomorrow."

The time was set and the couple left. Helen sat at her desk panting. She leaned back and wiped her forhead with a Kleenex. She was blinking rapidly—she put her hand over her eyes and made them close. "My," she said out loud. She tried to laugh. "My, my. What a silly girl."

That night she lay rigid in bed, her eyes closed, pretending she was sleeping. When she finally slept, she woke sitting straight up in bed, words still moving in the darkness. She lay back, her hands resting on her round stomach. Now she was afraid to sleep, but she passed into a silent, hollow dream that didn't free her until the watery gray light of dawn filled the room: Helen sat in a long, white room. Far away she heard solemn but jumbled words. Glancing around, she saw she was alone in the room. The funeral went on, static, interminable, and Helen sat in the pew talking to herself, her voice steady, droning, and after a while she realized the somber, incoherent words she heard far away were her own.

When Helen drove up in front of the house, just twenty minutes late, the couple who had come to the office yesterday weren't there.

Helen got out and went up the sidewalk to the house. They had probably left a note.

The mailbox was full of mail. Helen was taking the letters from the box when a woman opened the door. "Yes?" the woman said, looked at the mail in Helen's hands, then back at Helen and smiled. She was a lovely, slender, grayhaired lady. That was how Helen wished *she* looked. In fact, the woman reminded Helen of herself. Helen smiled at the lady, and into her mind fluttered the thought that perhaps this slender, happy woman was herself . . .

"Is that your car going off by itself?" the lady asked pleasantly.

Helen turned and watched her car move smoothly down the street. With a solid thunk it nudged the bumper of a parked car, caromed, and, rolling on, lumbered over a curb and headed deliberately for a tree which it butted into and stopped.

"Oh my," Helen said. Water poured swiftly through her head. She lifted a hand. The hand pawed air, and Helen watched it. The plump, pale hand was all she could see.

She lay on a lovely chintz sofa in a lovely room. The lady's name was Mrs. Pugerel. Helen heard herself talking. ". . . and Evie who is just the sweetest thing when I dress her in those little pinafores . . ."

She sat up and looked around. "What a lovely home," she said softly. "Such lovely gold sconces. And I just love the way they all harmonize, the walls, the gold molding along the ceiling. You wouldn't have trouble selling this house. I'm a real estate agent, did I tell you?"

Still talking, she rose. Mrs. Pugerel helped her with her coat and at the door Helen kissed Mrs. Pugerel's cheek. "You're such a dear," Helen said. "You look just like my Evie will look. I mean . . ." She laughed and shook her head. "My."

On the steps they looked down the street, the trees new-leafed and motionless under a sky in which a few placid clouds hung as if they had been pinned there so everything would look just right.

Then Helen remembered. "Oh my. I can't understand how I missed that house. This is Twenty-eighth, isn't it?"

"No, dear," Mrs. Pugerel said. "This is Forty-fifth."

"Oh. That explains everything. You know, Dr. Nye told me . . . I believe I will start carrying a little notebook with me at all times. Dr. Nye said I could expect . . . and I'm beginning to think he was right." She laughed. "I tend to be a little forgetful. I will be that way for a while. Do you know Dr. Nye?"

Mrs. Pugerel was inside and slowly shutting the door.

Helen walked carefully down the sidewalk and angled across the street to her car. Some children stood by the car. "Back away, kiddies. This will be dangerous. That tree might fall over when I back up." She glanced up the sloping lawn of the house whose tree her car had struck. The windows, reflecting the sky, stared blankly.

She got in the car, started it, and gripping the steering wheel, shut her eyes after giving the tree one last look. She raced the motor and backed away. She opened her eyes to see the tree still standing.

Helen swung out into the street and she had driven several blocks when the screaming voice of a child came looming from behind her. Had she heard the scream when she backed away from the tree? Had she in fact *heard* a scream?

"Oh my." She stopped the car, pulled into the driveway, and turned around. But she couldn't find the street—Was it Twenty-fifth? Thirty-third . . .?

She drove up and down looking at the houses sternly lining the streets, and each time she approached boys and girls playing she slowed the car almost to a stop, staring at them, while the children looked back at her.

She drove into the afternoon, no longer looking for the house with the tree, no longer stopping at each group of children. She drove on and on until, as though of its own accord, her car stopped at the curb in front of the small house on Logan Avenue where she and Rudolph had lived for thirty years.

That night after the little ones were in bed, Helen and Evie sat in the front room watching TV. Helen was talking and all at once she came quite close, for just a moment, to remembering something important from that afternoon. It involved death . . . Maybe on the late news . . .

When the news came on, she watched closely, not talking, but the news concerned the affairs of people far away. She watched the screen, nodding, and she was talking to Rudolph and Evie, and Helen watched herself rise and hurry out to the kitchen to get bowls of ice cream, and Evie was a little girl, and the three of them were talking and laughing while Helen watched, her lips puffing as she snored.

She woke in bed the next morning, opened her eyes, shut them, and saw the modern house on Twenty-eighth: gray, with massive square hunks of concrete boxed together like the building blocks of a giant child. She tried to forget the house, but it had moved into her and become not just a part of memory, but memory itself: the large white rooms where faces and voices become the past.

In the afternoon Mr. and Mrs. Taylor, the couple interested in seeing the house, met Helen at the office. Helen started to apologize for missing them yesterday, but they apologized to *her*—Mr. Taylor yesterday had been called out of town at the last minute.

So they loaded into Helen's car, and chatted as they drove along.

The Taylors were an interesting couple—maybe just the people to buy that house. Drake Taylor was rather impatient and nervous. He wore a little black hat, and craftily arched his brows, intently staring at Helen as she talked. Mrs. Taylor, pale and slender, laughed often and forcefully, stopping abruptly, expressionless, as if she hadn't laughed at all. She reminded Helen of Evie. Helen asked if they had children. "Yes," Taylor answered. "As my wife said, we have a daughter."

"Oh, yes," Helen said as if she remembered having been told. "How wonderful. Children are such a pleasure. Our Evie has been such a pleasure to Rudolph and me. And now her children, our little granddaughters . . ."

The day was exceedingly bright. Houses along the street shone in the sunlight, and the trees held themselves rigid, as if their brilliant leaves were glass.

"Have you lived here long?" Helen asked.

Taylor, riding in the front seat, looked out the window. Mrs. Taylor answered from the back seat: "We're moving here."

"Oh, yes. That's right," Helen said.

She drove on, talking rapidly. She interrupted herself to ask Mr. Taylor if he had happened to see a Euclid Avenue street sign.

"Back there," Taylor said low.

"Oh dear." Helen turned the car—making an approaching car swerve to miss them, its tires squealing. "People drive too fast," Helen muttered. She went on talking.

"*There*," Taylor said loudly.

"What?"

"Euclid."

"Oh. Well. We can . . . turn around."

"This is utterly . . ." Taylor started but Mrs. Taylor, leaning forward, cut him off with shrill laughter. "I do the same thing all the time," Mrs. Taylor said loudly.

Not talking, Helen carefully circled the block and got on Euclid.

"The house is on Twenty-seventh?" Taylor asked. Helen nodded. "Then it should be right up here," he said. "Twenty-seventh," he repeated slowly.

Helen nodded. "Twenty-seventh. Twenty-seventh."

"There!" Taylor said.

They made the turn.

"Now," Helen said. The Taylors sat back in their seats. "All the houses on this street are very modern. If you like modern houses, this is the house for you, and this is the neighborhood for you. Now here you see some of the modern designs." Taylor was looking out his window. He grunted.

"Now let me see . . ." Helen said, slowing the car. "1604 . . ."

"Up there," Taylor said.

They stopped in front of 1604, an English Tudor. There wasn't a for sale sign in the front yard. The motor idled and they stared at the house. "I don't think this . . ." Mrs. Taylor said cautiously.

"This obviously isn't the right street," Taylor said.

"Let me see . . ." Helen dug into her big purse. "I put the address and all the information . . . Here." She pulled out a note card. At the top was written in the precise script of Helen's hand before her stroke, "Reminder!" The rest of the card and the other side were blank.

"Well? Is that it?" Taylor asked.

"I don't think so," Helen said and stuck the card back into her purse.

"This is a waste of time," Taylor said. "Why don't we . . ."

"Drake," Mrs. Taylor said, her voice rising until it trilled into sharp laughter. "Let's try one street over."

Helen let out the clutch and the car lurched forward. They turned one corner, then the second, and as soon as they did, Helen felt water pouring over her head. Her arms became tremendously heavy and she gripped the wheel. She drove slowly down Twenty-eighth street. Her mouth was dry, her tongue thick. "I don't want . . ." she started, but choked. She tried to swallow. Finally all she could do was smile slightly.

At 1604 they found what at first glance was an enormous empty lot covered with trees and underbrush. But through the tangled landscaping gone wild they saw a high gray wall. The bushes at one time had probably been neatly trimmed; now they sprawled, grappling with one another. In the center of the trees lurked a leafless spine, a tree naked and guilty of death. A weed-clotted stone walk, with some steps missing, disappeared into the bushes and trees.

"Is this it?" Taylor said low.

Helen didn't answer.

"It's . . . *marvelous*," Mrs. Taylor whispered.

"Hmm," Taylor said. "I think I like it."

They got out and started up the walk. Taylor helped Helen and Mrs. Taylor where the stepping stones were missing. The earth was gouged and scarred in these places, and Helen recognized the narrow curlique roads of children's toy cars.

At the top they confronted the wall. Helen walked to one end, then the other while Mr. and Mrs. Taylor stood staring up it toward the sky. "There's no door," Helen muttered. "No door."

"Around the side," Taylor said. "It's on the other side."

"Yes," Helen said vaguely. Then emphatically, "Yes."

They followed a narrow path made either by children or dogs. High in the side wall, narrow vertical windows were cut in rows corresponding to the several storeys of the house.

"Isn't this marvelous?" Mrs. Taylor said.

"It's modern," Helen said, her head down.

She turned and called out, "Evie?" Her voice returned slowly from the far wall.

In another room the Taylors, talking eagerly, joined Helen. She nodded, though she didn't hear a word.

"Excuse me." She walked past them through the door. She turned right, then left at the next fork, hurrying. She looked in a room, said low, "Evie?" then went on down the corridor.

"Evie is at home," Helen said softly and nodded. "At home with Rudolph."

She turned back. Taylor was talking to her. She stared at his nose. It was quite large. His dark eyes were pulsing. "Aren't you feeling well?" Mrs. Taylor said into Helen's ear. Helen turned to her. "I didn't know you were there," Helen said, smiling. Mrs. Taylor's face was beautiful, soft, without lines, the face of a married woman in that time of life when there is beauty in everything that happens. "Do you have children?" she asked Mrs. Taylor.

They went on, Taylor talking, gesturing as he walked ahead, turning to make a point and glance at Helen and his wife.

"You have got us lost, Drake," Mrs. Taylor said, laughing pleasantly.

Helen walked away. After a while she stopped before a high white wall. She touched it, and it was cold. High, high above was the dim line where the wall touched the ceiling.

"Evie," she called and turned. Her voice bounced back sharply across the room and became louder with each brittle reverberation.

Walking between Mr. and Mrs. Taylor, Helen passed down a corridor. As Taylor talked he lifted both hands, palms up, as if lifting air. "How long have you been married to him?" Helen asked Mrs. Taylor.

At another fork the three went separate directions—Mrs. Taylor slowly walked up an incline, looking over her shoulder at Helen; Taylor turned and walked down the incline, looking he turned and called out, "Evie?" Her voice returned from the far wall.

n another room the Taylors, talking eagerly, joined . She nodded, though she didn't hear a word.

Excuse me." She walked past them through the door. urned right, then left at the next fork, hurrying. She d in a room, said low, "Evie?" then went on down the or.

Evie is at home," Helen said softly and nodded. "At with Rudolph."

he turned back. Taylor was talking to her. She stared at se. It was quite large. His dark eyes were pulsing. "Aren't eeling well?" Mrs. Taylor said into Helen's ear. Helen to her. "I didn't know you were there," Helen said, g. Mrs. Taylor's face was beautiful, soft, without lines, e of a married woman in that time of life when there is in everything that happens. "Do you have children?" ked Mrs. Taylor.

hey went on, Taylor talking, gesturing as he walked turning to make a point and glance at Helen and his

You have got us lost, Drake," Mrs. Taylor said, laughing ntly.

elen walked away. After a while she stopped before a white wall. She touched it, and it was cold. High, high was the dim line where the wall touched the ceiling.

Evie," she called and turned. Her voice bounced back y across the room and became louder with each brittle eration.

alking between Mr. and Mrs. Taylor, Helen passed corridor. As Taylor talked he lifted both hands, palms f lifting air. "How long have you been married to him?" asked Mrs. Taylor.

t another fork the three went separate directions—Mrs. slowly walked up an incline, looking over her shoulder en; Taylor turned and walked down the incline, looking

into sharp laughter. "Let's try one street over."

Helen let out the clutch and the car lurched forward. They turned one corner, then the second, and as soon as they did, Helen felt water pouring over her head. Her arms became tremendously heavy and she gripped the wheel. She drove slowly down Twenty-eighth street. Her mouth was dry, her tongue thick. "I don't want . . ." she started, but choked. She tried to swallow. Finally all she could do was smile slightly.

At 1604 they found what at first glance was an enormous empty lot covered with trees and underbrush. But through the tangled landscaping gone wild they saw a high gray wall. The bushes at one time had probably been neatly trimmed; now they sprawled, grappling with one another. In the center of the trees lurked a leafless spine, a tree naked and guilty of death. A weed-clotted stone walk, with some steps missing, disappeared into the bushes and trees.

"Is this it?" Taylor said low.

Helen didn't answer.

"It's . . . *marvelous*," Mrs. Taylor whispered.

"Hmm," Taylor said. "I think I like it."

They got out and started up the walk. Taylor helped Helen and Mrs. Taylor where the stepping stones were missing. The earth was gouged and scarred in these places, and Helen recognized the narrow curlique roads of children's toy cars.

At the top they confronted the wall. Helen walked to one end, then the other while Mr. and Mrs. Taylor stood staring up it toward the sky. "There's no door," Helen muttered. "No door."

"Around the side," Taylor said. "It's on the other side."

"Yes," Helen said vaguely. Then emphatically, "Yes."

They followed a narrow path made either by children or dogs. High in the side wall, narrow vertical windows were cut in rows corresponding to the several storeys of the house.

"Isn't this marvelous?" Mrs. Taylor said.

"It's modern," Helen said, her head down.

At the opposite end of the house another nearly impenetrable screen of trees and brush concealed a high blank wall. The Taylors backed into the bushes to appreciate the wall, while Helen walked along it.

"The door is around the corner," Taylor said confidently and led the way. Upon turning the corner they stood above what at first seemed a ravine but was in fact a driveway burrowed under the house.

"Oh," Helen said. "Yes. We go in through the garage door." She smiled. "See, I was right. There really isn't a door. Not a real door. Everyone goes in through the garage."

"I don't like that," Taylor said.

"Let's see it all before we decide what we like and don't like," Mrs. Taylor said.

Taylor led them down to the driveway.

Cut into rock beside the garage door was an oval steel hatch. Helen unlocked it and pushed with both hands. It swung open with a creak, and they stared into darkness.

Taylor dauntlessly stepped forward. He reached around the corner for a light switch but found none. Without hesitating, he disappeared through the door.

He was gone a minute, two, longer. Mrs. Taylor stuck her head in the door and called, "Drake? Isn't there a light somewhere?"

At that moment a light came on inside and Mrs. Taylor and Helen stepped into a white tile tunnel glistening under a blaze of lights.

"A big, roomy garage," Helen said uncertainly. "Very nice."

"It's the entrance way," Taylor said from atop a spiral staircase high above them. "The garage is back there."

Helen and Mrs. Taylor carefully climbed the staircase, and the three of them entered what reminded Helen of a hatbox. "Isn't this interesting," Helen said.

Next, the kitchen—glass, aluminum, glaring tile. "I *love* this kitchen," Mrs. Taylor responded. "I simply *love* it."

Into more rooms—high ceilinged, glea
rooms, small rooms that weren't actually ro
of angling passageways connecting room c
rooms, some windowless, some sliced w
windows high in the walls. "Why, there's no
Mrs. Taylor said.

"We're climbing," Taylor said eagerly. "
an incline. We're climbing to the second
"How many floors are there?"

Helen didn't answer, puffing, trying to
as they passed through room after identica

On the third floor the corridor forked. '
this house!" Mrs. Taylor said far away, and
"No," and followed to the right, walking alo
ing up its severe height toward the sky bey

Helen paused in the next room. If only
where she could sit for a moment. Or any k
would help so much if only there were some
look at. But the room was immaculately b
stared across the large room she realized th
dull silvery gray. She crossed the room, h
loudly, hollowly, and stood before the wall.
imperfect, and she couldn't see through th
room. "Isn't that interesting," she whisper
prised when neither Taylor nor his wife r
have gone the other way when the corridor
glass wall Helen saw a woman looking out a
said. She wondered if the woman was hers
hand—and the woman inside the glass lift
as if she were reaching for Helen's head. T
entered Helen's mind that if there was no c
woman couldn't leave. Squinting, she le
swirls in the glass prevented her from seeing
and from getting more than a vague impres
was a huge room, the largest she ha
goodness," Helen said.

slo
Hel
She
loo
cor
hon
his
you
turn
smil
the
beau
she
ahea
wife
plea
high
abov
shar
rever
dowr
up, a
Hele
Taylo
at He

up at his wife with a strained, quizzical expression; and before Helen took the other fork, she waved goodbye to them. She soon found herself before a high white wall, cold, and she looked up it to the line where the wall touched the ceiling. "Evie," she whispered and turned to hear her voice scuttling along the walls.

The Taylors came toward her down a wide incline, walking arm in arm and taking mincing steps. The couple were chatting silently. Helen knew they were far away and, though walking steadily with their rapid mincing steps, they weren't nearing Helen.

She started toward them, then, turning, she saw many doorways, more than she could count at a glance, lining both sides of a corridor. Slowly she sat on the white floor, tugging the hems of her coat and dress well below her knees and holding her purse on her lap. "My," she sighed. Her hands trembled. She caught her left wrist and tried to check her pulse. Maybe some aspirins. She dug into her purse and came out with a photograph of Rudolph, Evie, and herself, a picture taken when Evie was five years old. As she looked at it, the glare from the walls glinted on the shiny surface of the snapshot and abruptly they were gone and the house in the picture wasn't the little place on Logan Avenue in the summer of 1950, but a property for sale on the east side of town.

Naked, lean as a tree limb with its bark peeled away, Helen descended to sharp-angled, clicking corridors and doorways, a cold wind guiding her straight to Drake Taylor who stood, feet apart, beside his wife, his expression suspicious. As Helen approached, Mrs. Taylor backed away. Helen lifted her arms—they were young and thin and very long—and she put them around Drake Taylor's neck. Not closing her eyes, she kissed him and they floated back, going faster and faster, Drake Taylor beneath her, his eyes open, deep brown, serious, thinking the things a man thinks. Helen told herself she was Mrs. Taylor. "I will be her this once," Helen whispered. "But just once. I won't do it again, promise."

Not looking back, Helen left them. She would find herself.

A smooth wall revolved and Helen walked along it. She stopped before turning a corner and waited a moment. Then, prepared, she turned the corner to see what she knew she must see.

Helen Droosman, fat lady, lay on her back, her coat unbuttoned, the toes of her shoes pointing out.

Several young men bent over her, talking. One put his hands under her shoulders. Another gripped her ankles. They lifted her fat little body onto a stretcher. She heard them grunting.

They paused, stood, talked again.

Then they lifted the stretcher and their hollow footsteps echoed down the corridor. Helen heard one of them speak and the others chuckled. Their footsteps were now far away. A muffled bump carried down the corridors and through the rooms. Then silence.

Helen turned and immediately Mrs. Taylor came out of a room, speaking over her shoulder. From the same room came Taylor and then Helen, herself, her head bobbing in agreement as she listened to Mrs. Taylor. The three of them came down the corridor silently, though still talking, and it appeared all three spoke at once, nodded in unison, paused for a moment, then Taylor went on talking, gesturing with both hands. The three of them passed Helen and went on down the corridor. Helen went the other way.

Upstairs, she wandered through the white rooms. In the corner of a room she found a staircase and she climbed to the top floor of the house. There, in three small rooms, the windows were low enough for her to see out.

She saw clear across town, houses nearly hidden by trees, large buildings downtown.

Late in the afternoon Mr. and Mrs. Taylor and Helen climbed the stairs to the top floor and went through the three rooms, talking silently, each looking once quickly out the windows but concentrating on the rooms. Then they went back downstairs.

Far below, near the house, Helen heard the faint voices of children playing. She tried to look down the steep wall, but she couldn't see them.

The sun set swiftly and darkness slipped across town, hiding houses beneath trees meshed into a dark veil torn by streetlamps and dimmer, yellow light in the windows of homes.

Then it was night.

Helen stood by the window, waiting. Tomorrow would be her second day. But in a sense it would be her first.

PIZEOP

Mr. Logan, a small gray man, was sitting on the bed by the window, muttering and nodding at the sky, when young Dr. Youd breezed into the room. "*Good* morning, Mr. Logan," the doctor said.

As Dr. Youd glanced at Mr. Logan's chart, a nurse rolled a large metal cabinet into the room. "Shut the door," Dr. Youd said without looking up. The nurse obeyed, then plugged the cabinet's cord into the nearest wall socket.

"*All* right," Dr. Youd said and took Mr. Logan's wrist. He looked intently into Mr. Logan's eyes, then across his forehead, at his nose, his mouth. The features were softening with each treatment: Mr. Logan was dissolving to flaccid peace, his eyes as calm and unconcerned as a rabbit's.

"How are we today?" Dr. Youd asked. "They haven't tried to take you away, have they?"

Mr. Logan stared blankly at the doctor, as if he had succeeded in forgetting who *they* were. "When can I go home? Mr. Logan asked softly.

"Don't worry about that, my good man. You'll go home soon. And, by the way, Mrs. Logan is coming to see you this afternoon. That's good news, isn't it?"

Mr. Logan smiled vaguely.

"Ready?" Dr. Youd asked without turning.

"Yes, Doctor," the nurse said.

"All right." He started unbuttoning Mr. Logan's pajama top.

Mr. Logan looked down at the doctor's hands, his mouth opening with surprise.

When the shirt was open, Dr. Youd checked Mr. Logan's heart with a stethoscope, then leaned Mr. Logan back on the bed. The nurse stepped forward and applied a gel to Mr. Logan's temples. Around his head she strapped a gray headband which was wired to the cabinet. "Atropine," Dr. Youd said. She handed him a hypodermic and he injected Mr. Logan.

Dr. Youd stepped to the control panel of the cabinet and nodded to the nurse. She gently wedged a tape-bound tongue depressor between Mr. Logan's teeth. She moved away. Dr. Youd waited a moment, then threw the switch. Again Mr. Logan was jolted out of his skin.

Coming back wasn't easy—miles of empty fields to walk through. Far away, Mr. Logan heard people talking. He wasn't interested in what they were saying, and didn't suspect they were talking about him, though Mr. Logan was officially paranoid.

Coming back was enjoyable—even the gentle confusion which slowed him in remembering his own name. There was a lifetime of other details he couldn't remember, he supposed; Mr. Logan was aware but untroubled that he went so far away and took so long returning that each time he left more behind.

Whole days it seemed were spent in coming back, and Mr. Logan was glad. He even would have stopped and sat down for a while, but there were no rocks or stumps along the way, and he didn't have his body along to sit with. He had left it somewhere.

"Someday I won't bring anything back," he said, meekly interrupting his large wife, Bernice, when she visited him that afternoon.

"Of course you will." She patted his hand.

Bernice had no idea what he was talking about. Maybe he

was thinking of disappearing as he had several weeks ago, starting all this trouble. Where he had disappeared to, Bernice couldn't imagine. He had been gone for a week. On his next outing—as Bernice called them—he was gone three weeks. Both times when he returned he claimed to have absolutely no memory of where he had been, and there were no ticket stubs in his hatband or tattletale matchbooks in his pockets to give Bernice a clue, except after the second outing she found in his coat pocket a handful of sparkling white dust. After Mr. Logan's second outing he didn't go back to work, but slumped around the house. It was as if he had been all used up. Then one day he started jabbering at the windows in what Bernice described as beep talk, and she hustled him off to Dr. Youd.

Bernice gave Mr. Logan's hand another pat and went on talking. He sat on his bed staring in her direction. Occassionally their eyes met for a moment.

Two hours passed and Bernice got up to leave. She leaned forward as if she might kiss him, but stopped full face with him: "Any day now you're going to be well and then you can come home. Isn't that right?" she said.

He smiled into her large, middle-aged but unwrinkled face.

"Then everything will be all right again. No more funny business. Isn't that right?"

He nodded.

She patted his shoulder, tucked her purse under her arm, and started for the door.

Then Mr. Logan heard himself speaking: "Pizeop cheynep. Peirop te praperop pizeop."

She turned slowly. Her chin trembled, her eyes bulged. Then she regained control: frowning her eyes tight, she clenched a fist and lifted it. She didn't shake the fist but held it steady as though giving him a good look at just how large it was. "No more of that," she said. "No more. Do you hear?"

He nodded.

Squaring her shoulders, she marched out of the room.

*

The next day Dr. Youd came by, though Mr. Logan wasn't yet due for another treatment. The doctor's face was locked in an intent, precise expression through which he examined Mr. Logan. "*Do* it," Dr. Youd whispered.

Mr. Logan blinked. "Do what?"

"Beep talk. Go ahead. Let me hear you."

"I can't."

"Ah ha. You did when your wife was here."

Mr. Logan waited. "I can't do it now. I'm sorry."

"I see." Dr. Youd nodded slowly. "You don't have control of it. Right?"

Mr. Logan shrugged.

The doctor sighed and patted Mr. Logan's shoulder. "Time, Ralph. *Time* will do it." He leaned close. With his face in Mr. Logan's, he whispered distinctly, moving his sharp lips carefully as if he were inserting the words through Mr. Logan's eyes into his mind: "We will not let anyone or anything take you away. When you *know* that, Ralph, you may go home."

Mr. Logan smiled.

As Dr. Youd was going out the door, a sly grin flickered on Mr. Logan's lips and he said low, "Pizeop." The doctor didn't hear.

Mr. Logan turned to the window. Soon he was mumbling and nodding in agreement with the sky.

After a short convalescence at home, Mr. Logan returned to his job in men's wear in the department store. He was happy to be back, and though he was rather forgetful, he could still sell clothes.

Dr. Youd assured Bernice that Mr. Logan was cured. They could expect some fuzzy thinking, and he might be a little clumsy with the routine of their life. But the young doctor guaranteed that Mr. Logan would be Mr. Logan for the rest of his life. "What more could we ask for?" Dr. Youd said, beaming.

Bernice was skeptical. But at least she had him home again. Their children, married with families of their own, came by after supper a few times. Soon Mr. Logan's life was back to normal.

Then one day he left work in the middle of the afternoon. Under a blinding headache, that seared steel light into him as if the earth was screaming immense words across the sky, he somehow managed to drive home. Staggering through the front door, he was vaguely aware that Bernice wasn't home.

Suddenly the vast white noise and the headaches were gone. His head was filled with a hum.

He turned around twice. He went to the coffee table and squared the corners of some magazines. He stood before the fireplace and ran a finger along the mantle. Facing the front window, he saw out of the corner of his eye his left hand rising of its own accord to take an orange from a bowl of plastic fruit. His fingers slowly turned the orange.

"It's time now," he said, his voice unfamiliar, young and strong.

He replaced the orange in the bowl and walked out the front door. He got in his car and drove down the residential street, coming to a full stop at each intersection. He pulled onto the freeway and drove in the lane for slow traffic. Cars passed him silently. He looked straight ahead, watching the cars whiz by and shrink with distance as they went farther and farther away . . .

He mashed the accelerator to the floor. His car went so fast it seemed to float in the wind. Steering with his left hand, the other limp in his lap, he turned off the freeway and roared down an off-ramp. He blasted through a red light at an intersection. A glittering blur slid by the car as he raced down a narrow street where cars were parked in front of small shops. Then he was beyond the shops and speeding along a road through a flat stretch of land. Ahead was the railroad crossing, its warning light flashing. He saw the gray Diesel engine and the train approaching. He heard the train's baleful air horns, a long moan becoming louder and louder . . .

The car and the train reached the crossing at exactly the same instant. Mr. Logan didn't even close his eyes.

"A miracle." Dr. Youd shook his head. "He survived in spite of himself. Only because he was totally relaxed . . ."

"Relaxed," Bernice said.

"A depression such as his . . ." the doctor started, but again she interrupted.

"Ralph always was a weak man," she said.

Dr. Youd looked to the side, weighing this. "Perhaps. But what we must do now is prevent him from . . ."

"You and I see all this different." She looked squarely at the doctor. "He's only doing this so he can get out."

"Out?"

She nodded heavily. "He wants out of everything. You can call it paranoid or depressed or whatever you want to. But *I* know Ralph. All his talking to people in the sky and his outings and his crazy driving, they're all just tricks."

"Well . . ." the doctor said. Then he smiled glibly. "Perhaps you're right. At any rate, if he lives through this he'll need to be hospitalized. Do we agree on that?"

"I suppose he would like that." Her eyes tightened. "And I don't think I would mind it much myself." She nodded. "Yes. Maybe that's just the thing. Will I be able to visit him?"

"Certainly."

"For as long as he's in there?"

"Yes."

"Even if it's forever?" she said and her expression sank deeper into her face, solidifying into her future.

Dr. Youd saw the change in her face, saw it become the face of an old woman. He looked away and said, "Yes. Even if it's forever."

"When can I sign the papers?"

*

Mr. Logan spent his days in the recreation room—a large, high-ceilinged room filled, even on the grayest days, with light from grated windows set high in the walls. The recreation room echoed when only a few patients were in it, which was seldom the case; when many people used the room, noise babbled and rattled in a constant din. Mr. Logan roamed about watching the other patients, who either sat staring at television, or fidgeted at Chinese checkers and puzzles, or chattered with bright-eyed enthusiasm.

After supper, Mr. Logan and his roommates, three old men who years ago had decided on silence, retired to their room. At lights-out each night the old men promptly started snoring. Every week or so a ruckus drew Mr. Logan and his roommates into the corridor to watch the attendants scuffle with someone—usually the same persons. Mr. Logan looked on with mild interest.

All in all, it was a quiet life, a pleasant waning. Time stretched on and on like a vast field, one day swaying under and blurring into the next.

On Sunday afternoons Bernice visited. Mr. Logan's roommates obliged by wandering off single file down the hall, and for several hours Mr. Logan would sit on his bed while Bernice talked about their grandchildren and their neighbors. On one occasion, after Mr. Logan had been in the hospital for several months, Bernice seemed to lose track of what she was talking about, and started recollecting things she and Mr. Logan had done, and people they had known, thirty years ago. Mr. Logan stared off to the side as if he heard none of it.

Then one Sunday afternoon she started crying. Mr. Logan waited while she hid her face in Kleenex. After she stopped crying, she went on talking, but she left early, before the end of visiting hours.

The next Sunday Bernice came to visit wearing black. She talked slowly, leaning back in her chair, and Mr. Logan stared at her—at the black. He turned away. But the black again drew his attention.

Then Bernice took a pair of spectacles from her purse and put them on. Mr. Logan was fascinated. All her life Bernice had had the eyes of an eagle, and now she was wearing glasses! She was suddenly a stranger. He looked at her more closely.

The spectacles concealed her eyes with a sharp glint. Mr. Logan leaned to one side, then the other, but still couldn't see her eyes. There was something peculiarly familiar about this... Mr. Logan blurted out, "Have you always been who you are?"

She stopped midsentence, her mouth open. "What's that? What?"

He looked away. "Nothing."

"Say it again. Please."

"I just asked if you had always been . . ." He stopped himself, shook his head.

"I'm Bernice," she said, her voice quavering. "You don't think I'm trying to . . . *do* something to you, do you, Ralph?"

"No." Mr. Logan looked down. "I guess not."

"You shouldn't suspect *me*, of all people."

"All right."

She stared at him in silence.

"But you *are* different." He looked up. "Aren't you?"

She was indeed different. And it was more than the spectacles and the black dress. He realized Bernice had somehow become beautiful.

Always large, she now seemed positively colossal. The beauty which had eluded her all her life, now shone in the bulk of her person, in her very enormity. She had achieved the beauty of substantiality.

Bernice couldn't look at Mr. Logan while he waited for an answer. "Yes," she admitted. "I guess I am different. Because now I know something." She paused.

Then she went on. But not telling what she now knew. She instead talked rather aimlessly, as if she had had second thoughts in the pause. She ended on a firm note, once again in her customary direct, forceful tone, staring at him through the glasses: "You surely know I'm not one of *them*."

His eyes darted away. "One of who?"

"You know."

"I don't know what you're talking about."

"*Them*. Didn't they make you try to kill yourself in that accident?"

He shook his head. "That was just some bad luck."

They sat looking away from each other. The moment had passed.

Silence spread distance between them. They accepted it obediently, as if it were a natural force against which it would be stupid to struggle. Finally the bell rang, signaling the end of visiting hours.

Bernice slowly picked up her purse. She rose, huge. Mr. Logan stood. "I am still Bernice," she said. "You know that, don't you?"

"Sure."

They started for the door. Then Bernice turned and Mr. Logan was butted by one of Bernice's big, solid breasts. "I . . ." she said. Her eyes were invisible behind the spectacles. She was breathing hard. She moved her body against him and put her face in his.

They kissed. With their lips together, she was talking. "Come back. Please come back. I just can't live in that house alone." Through the glasses he saw her soft, powdered eyelids crinkling. "Please," she whispered. And then she spoke out loud, her voice deep, hoarse: "I am your wife. I have always been your wife."

Mr. Logan held her and they stood for a long time in the middle of the room. Then he pushed the door shut and guided her to his bed.

She wasn't Bernice, this immense, beautiful thing. He was sure of that. Bernice had been transformed. By desperation and, evidently, love. They lay with their eyes closed, their minds floating back and forth between each other. Here was life again, and from what now was his future there would be no coming back: the last of him, what remained, would be used up and he would be left with the last blurred winters and long, empty mornings. This future would be their life together as an old man and an old woman, the totality. And beyond that? . . .

Bernice held him in the ancient way. With their eyes closed, they kissed again and again.

After she left, Mr. Logan sat on his bed. Twilight settled in the hospital. The air was cold, and it soaked into Mr. Logan's clothes, into the mottled dry skin of the backs of his hands.

Another bell rang—supper.

Slowly he stood. He shook his head and spoke out loud: "It's almost done."

He went to the door. The patients had started their ragtag parade to supper. He waited until they all passed, then he stepped out and looked down the long corridor.

Someone was beside him. He at first thought Bernice had returned.

Instead, a thin young man, so short the top of his head came only to Mr. Logan's shoulder, stood looking up at him. His face was extremely narrow, and his eyes were set so far apart they were nearly on the sides of his head. He resembled a fish—a handsome fish.

Mr. Logan looked away. He would ignore the young man. He started down the hallway.

But the young man followed close beside him . . . and in a flash Mr. Logan was piggy-back on the young man and they were whizzing down the hall.

Mr. Logan giggled, then stopped himself. "I'd better get down," he said, but too low for the young man to hear, running hard.

Mr. Logan laughed out loud and leaned forward, holding tight as they went faster and faster.

*

After lights-out each night, they flew down the corridors. They never spoke. Mr. Logan told himself they didn't because the attendants would hear. Why the attendants might hear them talking, but hadn't heard Mr. Logan's raucous laughter, was a question he didn't bother with.

And each morning in the recreation room Mr. Logan and the young man were too busy to talk. Mr. Logan's intricate work with electrical components, which the young man produced from a cardboard box hidden under a big table in a corner of the recreation room, kept him busy all morning. His fingers flew, performing tasks with such speed and nimbleness that he was amazed.

In the afternoons, Mr. Logan retired for a long nap, and the narrow young man sat across the room, humming the same song over and over.

One afternoon Mr. Logan's nap was interrupted by a voice. He woke slowly, as if he were coming back through a wide meadow, hearing in the distance the firm, quiet voice.

But when Mr. Logan opened his eyes, the young man was silent, his mouth in its usual cryptic smile.

But Mr. Logan had heard the voice, and he had heard a word. Pizeop. Whispering the word, he closed his eyes and went back to sleep.

When Mr. Logan was released from the hospital, he retired from his job at the department store and sat home with Bernice. Their life was simple: they were old.

But Bernice wandered from day to day, forgetful, baffled, losing days. She cried, and Mr. Logan held her. In her sleep she wept with dread and joy, waking to kiss him and mumble words neither of them heard.

During the day they shopped and visited friends. Evenings they played bridge with the Wilsons, who lived behind them, and occasionally Bernice and Mr. Logan babysat with their grandchildren . . .

But in the middle of the night, alone, they again tensed to what Bernice knew was no longer *about* to happen but had started.

On a summer night they walked hand in hand in their backyard, the neighborhood silent and dark. They stood beneath the elm Mr. Logan planted several years ago. They strolled around the lawn in slow circles and then went back into the house. They made love again, beginning and ending, silent in the dark bedroom.

One dawn she woke believing birds were calling her name. She sat up, wide awake. Mr. Logan wasn't in bed.

She put on her robe and went down the hall. She looked in the other bedroom and the living room, but he wasn't there or in the kitchen.

Through the breakfast nook window she saw night slipping away, leaving the sky behind it new and gray. She turned to the window over the sink. In the backyard stood Mr. Logan in his pajamas, talking to a narrow little man beside the largest tureen Bernice had ever seen, a huge milk glass bowl that covered half the backyard. Mr. Logan was doing all the talking, gesturing with both hands, moving them up and down as if he were tapping balloons into the air. After a few minutes, the little man tilted back his strange narrow head and laughed. Then he reached up and patted Mr. Logan's shoulder, and they turned to the big bowl. They climbed a ladder up the side, and Bernice watched them disappear over the rim. The ladder withdrew after them.

Bernice's telephone was ringing . . . many phones were ringing, and the sound rose to a shrillness that froze the air, hardened the morning light, and Bernice watched the bowl lift gracefully, rising clear of the backyard fence and the elm tree. The bowl slid toward the Wilson house . . . Bernice gasped. But at the last instant the bowl skimmed the house, slicing so near the roof that the shingles fluttered. Darting for a point which Bernice saw for a moment as a dark coin in the sky, the bowl disappeared.

There followed a pure, massive silence.

*

Bernice wandered into the front room. She sat down and stared straight ahead. She knew now this was death: hard light, mystery, the sky filled with noise.

And he had left without even looking over his shoulder. She tried to cry.

But instead she giggled.

Dreadful. She covered her face with her hands and commanded: *Grief. Grief.*

But then she giggled like a girl, and before she could stop herself she jumped up from her chair and started dancing around the room, the floor shaking under her weight, tables and chairs bouncing.

She soon collapsed and lay panting, staring out the window at the sky, the shallows of the universe, where all things, including pizeop, swirled in constant, relentless meaning.

MRS. BELL AND HER DOG

The dog stood chained at the corner of the house. It looked back toward the alley, where Tyler peeked around the corner of the garage, but it didn't see him. It stood there—big, black, slick, its eyes intense. It turned and, dragging its heavy chain between its feet, went around the side of the house. Tyler waited. He knew all the dog's tricks. He waited for it to pop its head around the corner. But it didn't this time.

Tyler took a deep breath and stepped from behind the garage to the fence. With both hands he carefully opened the gate. He pushed it open slowly, then shut it after him, but he didn't hook it—in case the dog would suddenly come around the corner. The dog's chain was connected to an iron ring in the foundation of the house. It was long enough to allow the dog to reach the back porch.

Tyler hesitated a moment and then hurried across the yard to the porch. He reached the old wooden steps and he labored up them, holding onto the wobbly handrail, and then he was to the screen door of the porch and inside.

He paused, catching his breath, hoping for a moment that the dog would come around the corner and see that he had made it again, and he even thought of calling it—it didn't have a name, just "Yoo hoo" as Mrs. Bell called it, but that was what she called everyone. But he didn't want to taunt the dog. If he called it, it would come lunging around the corner, its great mouth open, its eyes furious, and it would see him standing up there on the porch inside the screen door. And then it would know he would be coming out again eventually, and Tyler knew the dog was capable of remembering and he also knew it was willing to spend an entire day just waiting around for him.

He crossed the sagging wooden floor of the porch and pushed open the door of the kitchen. He smelled the house's odors of kraut, dust, and old woman. He went in. The sink and cabinet were cleared, which meant Mrs. Bell was now in the front part of the big dark house. Or it meant—and this was even better—that she was next door to the two old sisters who also rented out a room or two. The old women gossiped and complained about the men they rented to—Tyler had heard them one afternoon when the sisters were visiting Mrs. Bell.

Tyler slowly and carefully crossed the linoleum floor and went into the hallway. Out of the kitchen, the house was cold. Dust was thick in the gray hall carpet.

He listened. He heard nothing—cold, deep silence. Which meant, he hoped and was almost certain, that Mrs. Bell was next door, for if she was taking a nap, as she sometimes did in the middle of the morning, he would hear her powerful snoring. There was a chance, though, that she was still in the house—that she had seen him come in and she was waiting for him to try slipping upstairs to his room, and when he was to his room she would come up behind him and yell so loud it would almost knock him down, "Well! What have we *here*!" and she would grin, all the intense, discordant features of her face exaggerated as she tried to open wider her small gray eyes. She always talked to him as though he were a child—he was certain she thought she could get away with it because she was old. He knew the type from other landladies over the years. They got away with a lot of things because they were old.

She hated the big dog. The tenant who had the room Tyler now occupied had given Mrs. Bell the dog as payment for three months back rent. The man had won the dog in a card game and he told her it was well worth the $75 he owed her. Mrs. Bell kept the dog because she couldn't find anyone who would give her $75 for it. Also, there had been a burglary three houses down, and Mrs. Bell had a terrible fear of burglars. She kept two loaded guns in her bedroom, she told Tyler soon after he moved in, perhaps as a warning to him.

She also hated the dog because it ate so much. With strange pride she told him the dog ate so much she had to buy day-old bread.

"Bet you never heard of a dog that ate bread, did you?" she said, her mouth crooked in a grin.

"No," he said.

"Well if you wanta see somethin' pretty peculiar, just bring yourself out here a minute."

He followed her to the kitchen. She went over to the big wooden cupboard under the counter and got out a big loaf of bread. "Day-old," she said and rapped it on the counter edge. It was hard. "Then I keep it a week or two. See? He likes it hard. Gives his teeth somethin' to do."

Then she got a big knife from a drawer and cut off the end of the loaf. "This is the *good* part," she said and went to the old ice box in the corner. She got out a package of wieners, took one and held it up for Tyler to see, and put the rest back. "*This* is what he likes," she said and walked slowly, heavily over to the counter and the loaf again. She picked up the big knife and after glancing at Tyler, her small eyes expressionless, she stabbed into the end of the loaf again and again. She panted when she was finished making the hole. Then she stuck the wiener in the hole. She waddled over to another drawer and got a slice of bread. "I gotta keep some fresh for this part of it," and she wadded up the slice of bread and stopped up the end of the loaf behind the wiener.

"Now comes the *good* part," she said and it looked like she winked at him.

She went to the back door. "Yoo hoo," she called and made a sucking *tch tch*. The dog came charging around the corner of the house, and Tyler held his breath. It leaped up the porch steps and reared on its hind legs against the screen door, and it was almost as tall as Mrs. Bell. Tyler knew the dog had seen him, he caught that moment when the dog's eyes were on him, a surprised moment, as if in its intense, hating mind flashed "*Him Him*" but then the dog saw the loaf as it stood reared up, its gaunt underside stretched before them—its sharp jutting ribs and the menacing thrust of its sex—the dog whined urgently and looked up from the loaf at Mrs. Bell and Tyler on the porch, and then Tyler realized Mrs. Bell was tee-heeing.

"D'you see that?" she said, turning and looked down at Tyler. "He smells the wiener inside it." Tyler nodded and looked away from her and at the dog again. There was an awful beauty in the dog—a valueless beauty, amazing, based on its intensity, its brutal thoughtlessness, its great size.

Then Mrs. Bell shoved against the screen door with her shoulder. When the door opened it pushed the dog backwards off the top step and it fell, a furious scrape and clatter of claws and stiff, long legs. But even as it fell, it kept its long-snouted, sharp head erect on its neck and didn't take its eyes from the loaf as it fell down the stairs.

She reached out the screen door and tossed the loaf into the air.

The dog, already to its feet again, jumped into the air and caught the loaf in its mouth with a loud *pow* as the teeth crushed into the loaf, and it dropped to the ground and stood, feet apart, its eyes staring ahead without seeing, as it choked down the loaf in three bites, with head tilted back, its throat bulging as it swallowed. It sniffed the ground for the crumbs and then looked up at Mrs. Bell and Tyler on the porch.

"Now that's somethin', ain't it?" Mrs. Bell said.

Tyler nodded and turned away from the door.

And maybe Mrs. Bell hated Tyler. And maybe that was to be expected. She said the usual cruel things—Did he get in for half-fare at the movies? Did he have a girl friend?—and all the time she was asking him she would stare down at him with those small dark eyes, like cinders thumbed down into wet earth. But Tyler had learned long before Mrs. Bell to seem not to be getting the point of things said by landladies, clerks in stories, and kids on the street. But with the dog, she played two things she hated against each other.

She could chain it to the front door of the house. Or she could shorten the chain so the dog couldn't come clear to the back porch steps. Tyler had complained. When he did she said, "Well now. I reckon you can use the *front* door just as good as you can use the back, can't you?" There was that glint deep in there in her eye: she knew he couldn't manage the front steps, that first day she had stood on the porch and watched him as he tried to walk up the steep steps alone. He had had finally to go up the steps one at a time, putting his suitcase two steps ahead of him and using both hands to hoist himself up onto each step. After he had got to the top, she told him he could try the steps on the back porch the next time, they might not be so bad.

But she wouldn't move the dog. She told him it wouldn't do any good to have a watchdog if it couldn't get to the door. "*That's* where the *burglars* will come *in*. The *back* door is the one you got to watch out for. You don't think they're going to come in the *front* way, do you?"

There were other things she did, too. When he first came to look at the room (that was before she got the dog), he noticed, first thing, that there was a key in the door of the room. He was glad of that. (The reason he had been looking for a new place to live was he had trouble with his other landlady. She kept coming into his room.) But then after he moved to the room at Mrs. Bell's he discovered that the key had disappeared. He asked her about it. She squinted and said, "Why, no sir. There's no locked doors in *this* house, believe you me. I just won't have none of that here. Everything's got to be on the up and up around her. That's just the way it's gonna be." And she knew he couldn't right then and there move out, for she had (*by mistake*, she said, the hint of a grin moving beneath the flesh caked on her face) opened a letter that came for him at the new address. Tyler had very efficiently changed his address well in advance of moving, and then the letter came to Mrs. Bell's before he had even moved in.

It was from his sister. She said she was sorry she couldn't send more money so he could have his furniture moved. And there was a check enclosed for his next month's rent, plus fifteen dollars for him to live on.

And another thing, on the first day of the month Mrs. Bell came into his room at six o'clock and told him she wanted her rent money. After the first time she did it Tyler tried to pay her on the day before, but she wouldn't take it. "No siree," she said loudly. "The first is on the first. If you give it to me sooner than that, it's an extra day on the other end, and that gets it all out of kelter. You got to remember, my friend, that I been rentin' out that room for twenty years. I know just *exactly* how to run my business, believe you me." And she did, too, for it was the next day that a bill collector tracked down for her the previous tenant and she got the dog for the back rent.

She came into his room just whenever she wanted to. To bring up a letter from his sister (the only mail he ever got). To see the windows were down when it was raining—like she thought he would sit and watch rain blow into his room.

He tried to push the big dresser oven in front of the door, but it was too heavy even with drawers out. There was a big overstuffed chair in the room, the bed, and the only piece of furniture he had been able to carry by himself from his other room—a small rocking chair.

There was no way he could keep her out of the room. And he couldn't confront her about it again. She would just stand there and bellow down at him, glee in her eyes and that little flesh-buried grin.

So he took it. There was nothing else to do.

He wrote letters to his sister and told her about Mrs. Bell, but he never sent them. He thought once of writing his sister a letter and going out and leaving it on the dresser where Mrs. Bell would see it when she went prowling around in his room. But it wouldn't do any good. When he came back Mrs. Bell would catch him on the stairs and yell at him again about all the doors in this house had to be unlocked at all times.

He had got a box at the post office and that stopped her

from reading the letters his sister sent him. It cost him a lot of money to get the box just for the two letters a month from his sister—his check, sometimes with a short letter, and the longer, monthly letter, a page and a half in which his sister always said the same things about her husband, who was a paper hanger, and her two kids in high school. But the cost of the mail box was worth it, and going to the post office gave him something to do.

That was where he had been today, and it was a good day, because he had got a letter from his sister.

He listened, and still heard no sound in the big house. He started upstairs, panting for breath after the first three steps. The rest of the way up to the second floor was an endless climb, and he started coughing from the dust he stirred up. He gritted his teeth and closed his eyes and climbed the stairs, knowing how far he had got without having to count the steps. When he was halfway up he stopped again, straightened up to hold onto the rail, and he was dizzy for a few moments. He turned around, for usually it was when he had got halfway up that Mrs. Bell appeared either at the head of the stairs—looming like a building—or yelled up from the foot of the stairs, for it was his coughing and gasping that let Mrs. Bell know he was going upstairs.

But apparently today she was next door. He sat down on the next step and rested and then, knowing she was out of the house gave him the strength to make it the rest of the way to the top.

He hurried down the hall by the door of an empty room, the bathroom, the enormous dark door of her room, then down to the end of the hall to his room. He went in and shut the door after himself. He looked to see if the key had reappeared in the lock. It hadn't.

He took off his jacket, sweater, and hat and put them up on the dresser. He got the letter from his jacket pocket and moved the rocking chair closer to the window. He sat down.

He looked at the postmark—Sheboygan, September 3, P.M. He looked at his sister's handwriting, the smooth, graceful way she wrote his name: "Mr. Larry Tyler."

He slowly tore open the envelope and slid out the two sheets of stationery. A page and a half. He looked at the second sheet to see that his sister's husband hadn't added a p.s. at the end. Once a long time ago his sister's husband had added a note to her letter. In it he said he didn't mind at all sending the money to Tyler because he knew Tyler would do the same for him. Tyler hadn't liked the p.s. The intentions were good, but he knew his sister had made him write it.

But this one didn't have a p.s. He started the chair rocking back and forth and he read the first page.

Dear Larry

How are you? Things here are fine I guess. Well as could be expected, ha ha! The kids are doing fine and we are all in good health. I hope you are in good health also, do take care of yourself. Do you need a new overcoat for this winter. Let me know that. Also be sure and get some more galoshes if you need them because this winter will be a bad one I have a feeling!

He paused before he went on to the second page. He had decided a long time ago he would never again buy clothes in stores. He would get a catalogue, mail in the orders, and have the things sent to his box at the post office. That would be better. He read the second page of the letter.

Your room sounds real nice, you are lucky to find such a nice room so close to the post office and grocery store! I sometimes wish we lived closer in to Sheboygan, but its nice for the kids here.

Let me hear from you. See you soon!

Sis

He read the letter again and then sat staring at it, not thinking except when in his mind he saw his sister's face, her lips moving, and he saw her laughing, silently as though he were looking at her through thick glass.

He folded the letter, put it back into its envelope, and folding it again, put it in his hip pocket. He got up from the rocking chair and went over to the overstuffed chair which he had scooted, his first day in the room, across from the bed with its back to the window. He took his shoes off and climbed up into the chair. He stood in the seat, leaning against the back, and stared out the window.

The view from this room was better than the one at the other room, but he didn't like it as much. He had told his sister he could see lots of trees and a street corner. The fact was, he could see more than that. He hadn't said that he could see the fronts of three houses, the entrance to an alley, and half-way down a side street. He didn't mention it because he knew she wouldn't have any idea what he meant. She might have thought she was supposed to feel sorry, and in her next letter she would say that Tyler had no idea how bad she and her husband felt about the way things were and so on.

It was a good window, but he didn't really like it. There were a lot of people to see, but they all seemed very strange. He couldn't get used to them. Maybe it was because of Mrs. Bell. She was turning him against watching them.

But he felt the same way when he first moved into the other room, and the room before that. It always took him a long time to get used to a new room and its window. And then one day, he hoped, he would be looking out the window and it would occur to him that this window and this room were all right after all. He hoped it would happen soon. But it wouldn't. Maybe it would never happen because of Mrs. Bell and the dog.

He watched a car drive down the street and slowly turn the corner.

He stood in the chair looking out the window for a long

time, not thinking, trying not to think, and now and then he spoke out loud, answering voices from memory. There were the time-softened faces of people he knew when he was in the handicapped school here in Chicago. He had had lots of fun in the handicapped school the four months he was there and he had known a lot of people there who would be his friend as long as he lived. He would never forget them. Sometimes he thought he would write a letter to Mrs. Gabree or Mrs. Malone or Mr. Holt who worked there. When he first left the handicapped school he thought about them all the time. And Mrs. Gabree came to see him a couple of weeks after he left the school. She told him she didn't like what she saw, because Tyler wasn't doing anything, and at the handicapped school he had learned some things to do so he could make his own way. But she was impressed that he kept his room neat and straight, and she saw that he still had all the small furniture that had been made for him by the others at the handicapped school. He would have written Mrs. Gabree a long time ago, except he was afraid that after she got his address she would come and see him again, and he would be embarrassed for her to come and see him now. And anyway, she probably didn't even work there at the handicapped school any more. That was ten years ago.

He heard a noise downstairs and thought at first it was just Mrs. Bell coming in the back door. But then he heard different noises. He got down from the chair and put his shoes on. His first thought was that someone had followed him back here and they were going to come up and get him, for sometimes when he went out people followed him around.

He listened. It sounded like there were a lot of people down in the kitchen. There was an awful lot of noise, a lot of feet, a lot of people hurrying around. He slowly went over to the door and put his ear to it. He held his arms in tight at his sides.

From downstairs he heard Mrs. Bell yelling.

Maybe a burglar had got in. Maybe a burglar had followed her. But wouldn't the dog stop a burglar? And Mrs.

Bell was still yelling in the same mean way she did when she was fighting with the dog. Tyler wondered who she had brought home with her that she would be talking to that way, and still there was a lot of noise of feet down in the kitchen. Tyler turned the knob on his door and opened it slightly.

The noise down in the kitchen abruptly stopped. Which meant Mrs. Bell and whoever was with her had passed down the hall to the sitting room. Now he could hear them better. He pushed the door open wide enough for him to stick his head out and see the top of the stairs. Then he couldn't move.

The dog topped the stairs, its bright black eyes fixed on his as if it had been staring at the crack in the door even before Tyler opened it wider, and Tyler stood there as the dog came down the hall as if it were gliding, its feet not touching the floor, and Tyler couldn't look away and with both hands he tried to find the doorknob, still unable to look away from the dog as it now passed the bathroom door, not running but trotting lightly on its stiff long legs, its lips curled back from its teeth, its tongue lolling out the corner of its mouth, hideous laughter on its sharp face, and he saw the chain dragging between its legs.

Still he couldn't move, couldn't even close his eyes, and then his hand found the doorknob and he drew his head back and the door swung shut with great slowness just as the dog reached it.

When the door was shut he heard the growling and he realized the dog had been growling as it came down the length of the hall. It scratched at the door, and its growling changed tone and went back and forth between a tight-throated, furious whining and an intense low snarl, a sound very much like the voice of a man.

Tyler backed away from the door, and he watched the knob. He was afraid the dog would—with horrible luck—strike the knob with a paw and turn the knob just enough to open the door.

He went to the side of the bed and started to climb up on it. He stopped. For what seemed like a long time he stared down at short, stubby arms, at his fat small hand gripping the bedspread.

Now the dog was scratching at the door. Tyler could see it, through the door, reared up on its hind legs.

He dropped down to his hands and knees and crawled under the bed, clear to the wall, and he backed up, looking out. He coughed from the dust he had stirred under the bed, and he put both hands over his mouth to stifle the coughing.

He lay on his side, looking at the floor of the room beyond the bed, and the scratching went on and on. Then he heard Mrs. Bell out in the hall yelling at the dog. The dog gave a sharp yelp and Tyler heard the clinking of the chain. Then the door opened.

He closed his eyes and put his hands over his face.

But he had to look. He spread his fingers and looked. He saw the dog's legs and sharp feet flashing black as it came into the room, and then the black hightopped shoes of Mrs. Bell as she came in. The dog ran from the door to the far end of the room. Then its face suddenly appeared as it looked under the bed. Its eyes and its face had knowing in them. The dog growled, both black eyes staring up. It lowered itself awkwardly and started under the bed.

All the while Mrs. Bell was yelling at the dog, "See, nobody's in here, get back, get back there, what are you doing?" and its head was under the bed, and Tyler lay very calmly. He moved his hips forward slightly and kicked the dog in the side of the head as hard as he could. But it wasn't hard enough. The dog just blinked its eyes, stopped growling for a moment as it snapped its mouth closed, as if to swallow, and then its mouth opened again, wrinkling its black face and squinting its eyes tight, and Tyler drew both feet up under him to stomp at the dog's face, and when he did—this time kicking with both feet as hard as he could—he closed his eyes, and it was like jumping into a deep hole.

And then he was screaming and grabbing with both hands for the bedsprings, for the dog had one of his feet in its mouth and it was shaking its head from side to side and snapping its mouth open and closed, trying to hurt, its eyes squinted nearly closed and looking up at Tyler's face now, right in the eye, and Tyler tried to kick the dog's head with his other foot, with the toe, aiming for the eye, and for a moment he heard his own husky, cramped voice yelling, "Stop it. Stop it," and far in the distance he heard Mrs. Bell yelling.

The dog's head jerked down into the floor and the outer edge of the bed lifted slightly as the dog's back was banged up against it, and Tyler's shoe came off in the dog's mouth as Mrs. Bell dragged the dog from under the bed by the chain.

He watched as Mrs. Bell kicked the dog, knocking it off its feet. It barked and then whined and snapped at her, and the shoe fell to the floor. Mrs. Bell kicked the shoe back under the bed, and Tyler stared at it as it lay on its side in front of him. It was wet. He held his nose to keep from sneezing and the dust was in his throat and lungs and he was going to cough, and he turned onto his stomach and pushed his face hard into his hand until he felt he was going to burst.

When he could breathe again, he turned his face to the side and saw Mrs. Bell's feet going to the door, and the stiff, resisting feet and legs of the dog as she dragged it out of the room.

Finally they were out of the door, then outside, and the door slammed.

He lay still, listening to her mumbling down the hall. He heard a door shut, then the heavy sound of her walking in the hall again, and his door suddenly opened.

"Yoo hoo," she yelled. "You can come out now. It's okay." She waited a moment, then he saw the door swing shut.

He reached over and got his shoe. He lay listening to the noises of the house. He heard her go into her room down the hall. He heard her talking to the dog. Then there was a long silence that was cut by the pure cold sound of the dog whining. She came out of the room again, and he heard and felt the diminishing shake of the floor as she went down the hall to the stairs and then downstairs.

*

He stayed under the bed until night. He heard Mrs. Bell come back upstairs and go into her room for the night. She had another fight with the dog. He heard her talking to it, then she yelled at it. The dog growled and barked and Tyler could even hear the powerful click as it snapped at her. Then there was the clinking of the chain and again the dog's piercing whine.

Tyler slowly came out from under the bed and climbed up into it, still in his clothes. He lay over against the wall, perfectly motionless. He pulled the covers over him, over his head. Now and then he pulled them down and looked out to see, in the light from the window, that the door of his room was still shut.

He got in the bed and took off his tie and shirt, but he didn't take his trousers off because he had to go to the bathroom and he didn't believe he could stand the moving around to get his pants off.

He lay awake, trying not to think, but the need to relieve himself became so great he had to get out of bed.

He stood in the center of the dark, large room for a while. He could risk going down the hall to the bathroom. But it was on the other side of Mrs. Bell's room, and he knew the dog would hear him. Mrs. Bell probably had her bedroom door shut. But he couldn't be sure of it.

His need to urinate was so great he had to hold himself, and for a moment he thought he would urinate in spite of himself, standing right there in the center of the room.

He thought of using the wastebasket. But that wouldn't work. And the window was too high, it would be dangerous, and someone going by, even if it was late, might look up and see him. Anyway, he probably couldn't open the big window.

He walked around in the dark room. For a while that helped, moving around. But then he had to stop and just stand there.

Then he thought of using the shirt he had just taken off. He reached over into the bed and found the shirt.

He hesitated. But there was nothing else to do. He held the shirt wadded and urinated into it. He gritted his teeth.

When he finished, he stood holding the shirt, his hand wet. He went over and hung the shirt on the back of the rocking chair.

He bent down and wiped both hands on the rug and, not letting himself think, he got back into the big bed.

Maybe tomorrow Mrs. Bell would go out again and take the dog with her. Or she would have the two sisters next door come over to her house, and with the two sisters here she wouldn't be afraid of burglars and maybe she would put the dog back outside.

The day after tomorrow she would go out, and when she did, she would take the dog back outside. He hoped she would. If she didn't put it back outside, he didn't know what he would do.

If she took it, he would leave the house and never come back. He would have to leave the rocking chair behind, but that didn't matter. It didn't look right anyway without the other furniture that went with it.

He would leave with just his one suitcase and he would go somewhere else.

Tomorrow, while he was waiting to see if Mrs. Bell was going to leave with the dog, he would write his sister a letter and tell her what happened. It would be a long letter. He would tell her everything. But not about the shirt. He would never tell anybody about that.

He would have his suitcase already packed and when Mrs. Bell left, he would leave too. He would go to the post office first, just to take a look to see for sure he didn't have some mail, and from the post office maybe he would catch a city bus, though he didn't like to ride buses because of all the people.

He turned onto his side and stared at the window. What if Mrs. Bell went out tomorrow and left the dog inside the house?

He closed his eyes but continued staring straight ahead into darkness. Finally he slept.

THE FUDGERS

Melody ran up the steps, bounced across the porch, and stopped inside the living room door when she saw her mother, in a clean apron, her hair combed, her spectacles shining like chromium disks, sitting with none other than Captain Catmun.

"Hello," he said. His voice was even deeper than on the tapes. "Do you know who I am?"

"Yes," she whispered.

His face didn't move but Melody believed he was smiling. "He's come to see you, Melody," her mother said. "Like he said he would someday."

"Yes."

"And he's brought some things, too." Melody then saw three opened boxes on a chair by the fireplace; she recognized the wrapping paper of a local department store. "Some nice things for our home. Isn't that just wonderful?"

"Yes."

"And something special," Captain Catmun said. Leaning stiffly forward, from inside his tunic he took a small object loosely bound in a maroon, green, and black silk scarf. "Here."

"Go ahead, Melody," her mother coaxed. "It's okay."

Melody took it and was surprised it was so heavy.

Captain Catmun slowly turned to Melody's mother. "Something special, for her. Something I brought back just for her."

Melody's mother nodded. Then—"Oh." She jumped up. "Sure. I'll just go fix some lemonade." She trotted out.

"Now," Captain Catmun said. "Go ahead." His face was strained but not completely impatient.

"I'll open it later," Melody said. "After supper. That's when I usually open things."

He shook his head. She was looking right at him but she couldn't see his eyes. They were shaded by his sharp, protruding eyebrows. She wondered if he really had eyes. Melody wondered why she wrote him all those letters. Maybe his eyes were rocks. "Go ahead," Captain Catmun said. "Open it."

She looked down at the gift. The maroon, green, and black seemed moving against each other slowly, wetly. "I kept all your letters," Melody said.

And it worked! He stared at her, his hard sharp lips parted but silent.

"And I took the tapes and played them in home room. They thought it was really neat." Melody smiled her best smile, the one that made her cheeks round and mischievous, and made her eyes sparkle. She could actually feel them sparkling, and if she smiled this way too long she got dizzy. "Did you keep my letters?" She hadn't meant to ask that, it just popped out.

"Every one," Captain Catmun said low and raspy. "I read them each night before I go to bed."

Melody didn't actually like that, but she continued smiling. "Neat," she said.

She was sure Captain Catmun was about to tell her again to open the gift, but just then her mother came in with a tray. "Here we are!" She poured a big glass for Captain Catmun, the ice cubes tinkling with that snug, cooing sound they make in living rooms everywhere. She poured some for Melody and, as she handed it to her, saw the gift.

"Oh my! Isn't that just lovely"—and she took it from Melody's hands, for in fact Melody lifted it, subtly and so imperceptibly that no one but her mother could have seen she was offering it to her. "Oh, you haven't opened it. I came back too soon. Oh, I'm sorry." She turned to Captain Catmun. "I interrupted. Didn't I?" Melody watched her mother's hands as she talked; her fingers were giving the silk scarf little squeezes, trying to tell what was inside. Her mother turned, glanced at Melody, and instead of returning it, put it on the table and sat down. She smiled at Captain Catmun. "That's so nice of you."

"I think she will like it," Captain Catmun said.

"Of course she will," her mother said, smiling an older edition of the same smile that was such a big success for Melody. The smile squinted up the mother's eyes and curled the corners of her mouth. This made a lot of lines that resembled cat whiskers. Sometimes Melody's mother looked like a large cat wearing spectacles and smiling at people in the living room. "We had an article in the *News* about you."

Captain Catmun moved his head slowly up and down. "Melody Ann sent me the article," he said.

"Melody Ann!" her mother said. She cat-smiled at Melody. "I haven't called her that in years. I believe I'll start calling her that again." She leaned forward. "Hello, Melody Ann."

Melody stared back at her. "Hello, Mother." Then out the corner of her eye she saw Captain Catmun doing something. She turned quickly and he was reaching into his tunic; he drew out a cardboard cylinder three feet long. He tapped the mother's hip with one end of it and she turned, her eyes very big.

"For you." He slid the cylinder under her arm and across her lap.

"Oh my," she said. "You're so generous. Why, it's just like Christmas." She looked at her daughter. "Isn't this just like Christmas, Melody Ann?"

"Yes, Mother. Just like." Melody slumped back in her chair, extending her legs before her and crossing them at the ankles. Captain Catmun was facing Melody's mother, but Melody was sure his eyes were on her own thighs. Did he approve?

Her mother was opening one end of the cylinder. Melody was staring at Captain Catmun, and she was certain he was staring back at her. "Are you really Captain Catmun?" Melody said.

At the same time Melody spoke, her mother pulled from the cylinder a roll of paper, and said loudly, "Oh my! Would you look at this!"

She carefully unrolled crinkly salmon paper, kept unrolling it until it covered her lap and extended down on the floor for several yards. "Well, my goodness. There's just no end to it."

Melody looked into the paper's intense lines and creases. She squinted, then said, "That's a *ho tuy.*"

"What's that?" her mother said, still unrolling it. It was all over the living room floor now, rippling and creeping as if on its own or as if little creatures were under it carrying it along.

"*Ho tuy,*" Melody said over the noise of the crinkling, rustling paper, and again—"*Ho tuy*!"—gleefully, rising at the same time Captain Catmun pushed himself up from his chair. Melody leaned down and touched the paper. It was soft, lively, squirming under her touch, burning her fingertips pleasurably like hot sand, and, bent over, Melody felt Captain Catmun behind her—he gave her a little shove and she tumbled forward with a shriek onto the *ho tuy.* In the distance she saw her mother fling off her apron and flip her spectacles clear across the room onto the mantle. She brightly blinked and opened her mouth wider than Melody had ever seen her open it. Her mother yelled, "Here he comes!" Melody turned as Captain Catmun, his tunic unbuttoned all the way and flapping like wings, dived over her shoulder into the *ho tuy* and he was a great glittering flash, a large metallic contraption, complicated, impossible, and beautiful.

*

Ron honked out front then came up on the yard and yelled and then pounded on the front door and finally came right on in and was standing in the living room when Melody appeared at the head of the stairs.

"What's? . . ." Ron said. Melody was naked. Ron looked away. "What's happening here?"

Melody shook her head.

"What's all this?" Ron said, looking around the room.

"It was *ho tuy*. But none's left."

"Gee, Melody," Ron said. "Why'd you *do* all this? Everything's torn up. Wait'll you mom sees this."

"It was Mother's idea." Melody leaned forward and fell down the stairs.

"Gee." He carried her to what was left of the sofa and sat down with her on his lap. "This is really terrible." He sneaked a look at her breasts. Then he looked around the room. "I don't know what to do." His eyes passed, then returned to the corner by the fireplace. He whispered to Melody, "Is that your mother?"

"I don't know." Melody's eyes were closed.

"Yeah. It's her," Ron said. "It don't look like her, but it's her."

"Ten-*hunt*!" Captain Catmun stood at the head of the stairs. He wore his tunic and trousers, but he was shirtless, barefooted, and his toupee was on sideways. "You and I are going up front for maneuvers."

Ron shook his head. "I just came over to see Melody."

Captain Catmun came slowly down the stairs and nodded toward the front door. Ron scooted out from under Melody and stood. "But I told my mother I wouldn't be gone long."

"Just a little work-out," Captain Catmun said. "A few maneuvers." Ron sighed and preceded him out the door.

Melody sat with her eyes closed and far off heard Captain Catmun hup-hupping. After a while she went to the window. Captain Catmun sat smoking a cigar in a lawn chair, his legs crossed, while Ron marched up and down. A little boy and his dog ran along beside him.

Melody turned and headed through the rubble for the kitchen. "Come on, Mother, let's eat breakfast."

They were at the kitchen table when Captain Catmun and Ron came in. Ron was sweating and had taken off his shirt; his face was flushed and bright. He laughed and said loudly, "We sure had a work-out, you know that?"

"Good," Melody said. "We sure had a breakfast."

"Good," Captain Catmun said. "Come on." The three of them followed him into the living room. He lit a cigar and handed the maroon, green, and black silk-bound gift to Melody. "This will mean more to you now," he said.

"I bet so," Melody said earnestly. She squeezed it a few times and it responded smoothly, lumpily. Melody laughed. "I'm afraid to open it."

"I'm afraid, too, all of a sudden," Ron said.

"Go ahead," Melody's mother said, standing behind them.

"Should I?" Melody asked Captain Catmun.

He nodded and, tilting back, shot a smoke ring through a hole in the ceiling.

Slowly, delicately, Melody untied a sinewy knot—then another. And another. Captain Catmun, her mother, and Ron waited while she untied knot after knot, peeling back each maroon, green, and black flap as she untied it. Soon her lap was covered with flaps like the huge petals of an exotic blossom. With the last knot untied, Melody picked it up and held it in the palm of her hand. It looked like a lump of yellow fudge. She turned to Captain Catmun. She believed she saw his eyes, and she believed one of them winked.

"I don't get it," Ron said.

"Here," Melody said and tossed it to him. He caught it with a soft splat, and it became slightly larger. "Oh," he said. He squeezed it with the fingers of both hands and it grew slightly. "Gee."

"Let me," Melody said and rose, the silk sliding off her

legs with a whisper. She took it from Ron and cupped it in her hands. She pressed it with her thumbs. "See," she said softly. "A little at a time. Not all at once."

"Roll it," Ron said, and Melody rolled it gently between her palms; it became gradually oval.

"Well," Melody's mother said. "I see how it works now."

"Not altogether, you don't," Captain Catmun said.

They turned to him. His lean face was expressionless. "There is one other aspect you haven't yet looked into."

" 'Looked into,' " Melody whispered. She pressed in her thumbs and pried it open. Small and precise, it smiled and on its own opened wider and said, "Ah pinu on lequey?"

"Larger," Captain Catmun said across the room.

Melody gave it a squeeze. It increased in response; it was now roughly the size of a small head.

"*Pi*nu. Pinu on lequey."

Again she squeezed.

"Let me do an eye," her mother said. She reached over and jabbed in her thumb. Under the mouth, Ron tickled forth a throat. The mouth, smiling, chattered away.

By noon she lay on the sofa, flat on her back, talking non-stop, though after a while they stopped listening. They congratulated each other, ate lunch, and came back into the living room. With what remained, a pinch left over from when they had decided to make her a woman, they started another. Melody's mother put the extension in the table for supper and still there wasn't enough room for everyone, so they ate buffet, all the while talking and laughing. After supper they roamed about the house, poking into things and familiarizing themselves, trying on clothes, listening to the radio.

Captain Catmun sat in the front yard in his tunic and an old pair of Bermuda shorts. Sometimes he wore his toupee, sometimes not. He smoked cigars and talked to passers-by, and in the last week of August he walked down to the college and got a job. Using his newly acquired influence, he got

Melody, Ron, and all the others accepted as special students.

When school started, the neighbors would watch Captain Catmun, carrying an old leather satchel, walk by in the morning, then later Ron would come by and pick up Melody. Then all the others, walking in twos and threes, talking and gesturing, would go off with their books and sack lunches. The neighbors easily overcame their initial suspicion, for, after all, the newcomers were so friendly, they always waved as they went by and even called hello if you gave them the least chance, and by Thanksgiving they hardly had any accent at all!

ON THE EMPEROR'S BIRTHDAY

I was editing a literary magazine in Sachs Harbor, Canada—on the Baufort Sea, Banks Island's only town. I could name some of the folks, we could go look in the windows at them around their shortwave sets, listening to the world . . .

I lived aboard the schooner *Tuktoyatuk Scheme*, which ran aground and froze solid longer ago than the oldest-timers in Sachs Harbor can remember. I dragged in a stove, insulated the captain's quarters with books and manuscripts, and stocked up on bacon, beans, and my favorite, *ropnung*, Sachs Harbor's oily fudge.

The supply and mail ship came in spring, when the sun, small and yellow, appeared with the tainted shyness of a used debutante, and again a month later, just before winter fell like a wall. I never actually saw the supply ship: the bay at Sachs Harbor was a great rubble of ice, jumbled hunks big as apartment buildings, with a zigzag trail chiseled through, along which supplies and the mail were packed in.

Some nights I would hear the ice grinding and crunching. I would run topside and shine a light across the bay—and see nothing but those fifty-foot molars. It was only when I wasn't looking that they would grind in the agony of some geologic indigestion a million years past. Or maybe they were sleep-talking a glacial dream of movement. My own sleep rumbled, shook: giants, their backs always turned, lumbered off with tons of ice on their shoulders, carrying it worlds away to the sun.

I sat deep in the *Tuktoyatuk Scheme* smoking cigars and reading manuscripts. When I had enough good stuff, I'd pack it up and, come spring, fire it off to the printer, a cheap operator in Vancouver. He would, in time, send me the galleys, I'd correct them, return them, and, in time, I'd receive the latest issue of my magazine! Next I sent copies to subscribers—a tricky task, for my readers (writers, poets, and other lit mag editors, and their wives, mothers, and sweethearts) moved every two or three weeks, if not oftener, literary Bedouins, their gaunt camels burdened with lyrics, short stories, novels ... When I got back a copy of the magazine that had been a couple of years in the mail, following a subscriber hither and yon before a little red *Left No Forwarding Address* at last sent the magazine, crumpled though unread, its envelope in shreds, home again, I would open the magazine and look through its familiar pages, hoping and half-expecting to find a record of its journey—a story, a poem or two, on how a subscriber ceases to exist.

I sought new subscribers by writing crafty letters to strangers, and I tried to promote "casual sales"—a fellow wanders into the store down at Whitehorse, sees a stack of my magazines up on the shelf and plunks his money down for a copy!

Between issues, I work on my own stories, and sometimes I'm so deep into it all I fail to hear footsteps on deck—for believe it or not about once a year someone from Sachs Harbor comes out and looks in on me.

Sometimes the opposite happens—I'll be working away and hear a scuffle up there and when I shinny up and peer across the deck, there's nothing. Wall on falling wall of snow and wind, vaster than the long emptiness we try to prepare for by closing our eyes . . . *It'll be like this forever, nothing, without words, without even thought* . . . Though when I try that I usually see a street corner, a post office with people hurrying in and out. Or a tropical forest with a goggle-eyed leopard smiling from a tree, a giraffe craning in elegant profile over the hump of an elephant who poses, head lifted, trunk curled—and off to one side, almost out of view, a bunch of naked little people hurrying down a path, the last one looking over his shoulder, his eyes gleeful, his lips moving with words I can't hear.

But my guests from Sachs Harbor invariably come right on down and will be standing behind me, looking over my shoulder, before I realize they're there.

I spent sixteen years this way.

By the second mail which that year slipped out just inches ahead of winter's grab, I sent the latest issue of the magazine, and celebrated with a cigar and brandy. I was luring forth fond memories from the crank-up Victrola the *Tuktoyatuk Scheme*'s captain had left behind, along with some records. My current favorites were Caruso singing *Celeste Aida*, and a chorus of young ladies doing *Ta-ra-ra-boom-de-ay!* I was at my desk chirping away on my machine, when the most extraordinary thing happened. I threw the carriage for another line, and the typewriter flew across the cabin!

Then I flew after it.

On my way back I grabbed the leg of the desk, which was bolted down. The deck under me—*Tuktoyatuk Scheme* herself, all of her—tilted with a great cold creak of timbers that I recognized immediately, though I had never heard it before.

The wheel!

Get topside! Aim the damned thing before she crashes into the ice!

By the time I reached the ladder, made it to the top, and poked my head out, the *Tuktoyatuk Scheme* was clipping along as if under full sail, cutting through the night just as if she knew where she was going, just as if the old captain was at the helm taking her at long last by God out of this frozen lake of Hell!

And the bay was no longer a locked yap of frozen teeth, but a true bay—a sea!

She cut through black water and the wind crashed waves across the deck, washing down the hatch where I stood. I gave up the notion of steering her. I went down and set to securing my typewriter and everything else that was dancing around. Then I sat in my swivel chair and tilted and swung as the ship rolled on. I had paper, beans, and booze to last a lifetime.

And I discovered I was one of those fortunates who can ride high seas without getting seasick.

I counted days for a while, then gave up. I'd never see Sachs Harbor again, no sense kidding myself. Wouldn't get to read the mail responding to the latest—and final, alas!—issue of my magazine. The *Tuktoyatuk Scheme* steadied, smoothly riding some great current, but I was in such a funk I didn't leave my cabin. Would we go clear to the other pole? Freeze up all over again and wait a hundred years till another unnatural thaw freed us, another unexplainable current carried us on . . .?

When I finally went topside, I saw a large thing in the sky. It was the sun. The day was mild, a long mild morning. The sea was green, with low languid waves suggesting things untoward and frisky.

I took off my shirt.

Exploring the *Tuktoyatuk Scheme*, frozen shut all these years except for my quarters, I found casks of dark water. No telling how long it had been in those casks, frozen hard as granite. I found some tin cups down there, a thousand or so, and gave it a taste. It was the finest I ever drank!

I found bales of bright pennants and jaunty flat caps. And bell-bottom trousers which I put on and girt tight at the waist with rope—there was enough rope aboard for a million belts. And a crate of big ledgers. I straightaway took one topside and began a log.

One day I was in the crows'-nest, a barrel which I suppose had been put up there after the *Tuktoyatuk Scheme* ran aground, the old captain hoping that from atop the mainmast he might spy the open sea, or sooner smell the thaw that would free his ship. I was up there scribbling away when a great chill breathed on me, as gray as the sleep at Sachs Harbor. We had sailed into such a soup that when I looked straight down, I couldn't see the ship.

I stayed a while, gliding along with nothing above me, around me, or below, but got cold and climbed out of the barrel. I hugged my way down the mast, stopping several times and listening. I got the eerie feeling there was no bottom, that I'd just keep going down until I reached water . . .

On deck, I felt my way to the hatch and went down to my cabin and lit the lantern. I ate supper and finished off the entry in the log—*Fog!* underlined twice, my pen scratching loudly. I turned down the lamp and tiptoed to my bunk. I lay there listening.

The ship shuddered. I woke—it was day. Again something bumped her and there was a loud scraping along starboard.

Feet hit the deck. The hatch opened, they came down the ladder. The cabin door banged open.

In came two small men, one gripping a rifle. They wore faded gray uniforms, smooth as silk and hanging loosely on their narrow shoulders. At first I thought they were old men, but their faces had a glassy, unwrinkled smoothness like teacups. Then a third man entered, a small fellow in green skivvies, and a dishpan helmet pulled down over his eyes. I soon learned he was their captain. He had that same smooth absence of expression. The three of them searched the cabin, tossing manuscripts around, banging open drawers. They glanced in the general direction of each other—at the smooth brass buttons down the fronts of their tunics, and at the captain's bare feet. The captain spoke.

I shrugged. "Sorry. I don't speak . . . Japanese, is it? I'm an American, Hobart Stull's the name. Most recently from Sachs Harbor, Banks Island, Northwest Territory, Canada. I don't have a rank or serial number. Sorry."

The captain uttered a low sushing sound. They marched me topside where I saw a gray warship, narrow as a dagger, tied alongside the *Tuktoyatuk Scheme*. This was the *Hidari Maru*, a destroyer. They took me aboard and put me below in a tiny compartment. I sat there several hours before they came back and took me to the captain's quarters.

I was made to kneel before a table where he sat in full but faded uniform. Behind him stood a small, especially seedy fellow. Piled everywhere were manuscripts they had taken off the schooner. The captain spoke. The seedy fellow shuffled forward and said, "Okay, Joe. Fujiwara-san says you're a writer, eh?"

I nodded.

"What do you write about, eh?"

I shook my head. "I . . . don't know."

The translator squinted, then turned to the captain and passed this on. The captain spoke and the translator said, "Fujiwara-san says it appears to him your themes are fooolish adventure and clown love." The captain spoke. "And foolish grief and clown redemption. Whaddya say, Joe?"

I nodded. "I guess he's right. Tell him thanks."

"Okay. And who are all these other guys?"—motioning to some manuscripts in manila envelopes.

"Contributors to my lit mag."

This pleased Captain Fujiwara. He leaned back and smiled with such obvious slyness and cunning, I couldn't bring myself to be wary. "You publish the work of others?" he said through the translator.

"Yes. It's my duty and pleasure. As you command a mighty warship, I humbly navigate a lit mag through the choppy shallows of our times toward the wide sea of posterity."

The translator didn't fly into this but broke up laughing. Captain Fujiwara was laughing too. He spoke, and the translator laughed harder. "What's that?" I said.

"Fujiwara-san says you and the bosun are from the same worm jar. You whistle *Dixie*."

Fujiwara and the translator spoke, glancing at me as I knelt there, smiling idiotically. Then Fujiwara spoke in English! "I believe you're a good fellow, Hobart Stull, but you must now tell me if you are a Roosevelt spy."

I assured him I wasn't.

Fujiwara sighed, leaned back, staring off, and began a hazy lecture on naval strategy, a carefully uttered but withal dreamy discourse, as if he couldn't believe all of this, though I was obviously willing to buy the whole works. He analyzed the events that long ago led to his launching this maneuver, and with fervor he commended the dedication and great fighting spirit of the *Hidari Maru*. Toward the end, he touched on victory.

The translator brought a large photograph album and put it on the manuscripts. The translator brought me a chair, and for several hours Fujiwara talked and turned the pages. There were his crew when their uniforms didn't hang loosely, and there was the *Hidari Maru* when she was new, looking exactly as she did today—she hadn't changed at all. There was the Emperor, followed by pages of women, children, old people. Fujiwara turned these pages without comment and at the end came to a photo of a young officer, Fujiwara himself, staring out. Fujiwara spoke again of strategy, divulging that his forte was in waiting: the fact that while riding at anchor he had seized a ship (the *Tuktoyatuk Scheme* had traveled thousands of miles to find the *Hidari Maru* and slide right up alongside her) vindicated Fujiwara! But the time would come when he would make his big move. At the right moment the *Hidari Maru* would enter the heat of the fighting. Until then, Fujiwara and his men must wait at anchor in the middle of the Pacific.

The translator served a light lunch of fish in thin scrolls of seaweed. As we were eating, I said to Fujiwara, "I confess, I sometimes have doubts." He stared at me, then looked away. "All in all, there's really nothing else for me. You at least have all these other people—your crew."

He frowned. "What exactly are you meaning?"

"Why, I am . . . telling you things I've never told anyone else, that's what."

He squinted, picked a bone from his teeth, looked at it, dropped it on his plate. "Why do you tell me these things?" he said.

"Because you told your secrets—military secrets, at that. So in return . . ."

He chewed rapidly, swallowed loudly and with difficulty, then made the same intense sushing sound I heard form him earlier. He struck the table with his fist.

"Sorry I mentioned it," I said. "I merely . . ."

Fujiwara shouted in Japanese. The translator snapped, "Shut up, Joe." Fujiwara spoke again. The translator passed on—"Stand up." I stood. He kicked the chair away. I knelt before the table. Fujiwara looked down at me and spoke slowly, his teeth clenched: "You have steamed your geese, Roosevelt Stull."

I whispered, " 'Cooked my goose.' "

"That doesn't matter," Fujiwara shouted and delivered a crashing blow to the table and stood leaning on the fist as if he would press it on through. "You have out-stuck your neck and now . . ."

I waited. The moment stretched. I breathed. I heard Fujiwara breathing on the sly. I felt the gradual rise and fall of the ship.

Fujiwara straightened, nodded to the translator. "Stand up," the translator said. I obeyed, and he scooted the chair up to the table. I sat down.

"Under these circumstances," Fujiwara said, "you will become a crew member of *Hidari Maru.*"

"Oh! That's . . ."

"Shut up, Joe," the translator said.

Fujiwara went on. "You will serve in a literary capacity."

From his tunic he took a small, frayed notebook and slowly leafed through it, looking at both sides of each page. After a while I believed our business was finished, that Fujiwara would read for the rest of the afternoon. Then he came to a page which he read twice, then turned it and looked at its reverse, which was blank. He carefully tore the page from the notebook. He took a pen and ink from a drawer and with his left hand, precisely drew an X through the page with writing on it. On the backside he commenced writing. Soon the small page was covered with dense columns. But in a corner at the bottom there remained space for Fujiwara to dot a short line. He laid the limp little page on the table before me and put his pen beside it. "Sign there," he said and touched the corner with the long fingernail of the little finger of his left hand. I wrote as tinily as I could, filling the corner with *Roosevelt Stull.*

Fujiwara jumped up and at the top of his lungs gave a speech. When he was finished, the translator tapped me on the shoulder and nodded toward the door. Going up the companionway I asked him what Fujiwara had said at the end.

"That you're the ship's writer."

"What's my rank?"

"There's no rank to being ship's writer. It's a mere distinction. Once or twice a year there's honor."

"Well. That sounds pretty good."

Topside, the crew were carrying off all my rope, books and tin cups, and rolling my casks of old water aboard the *Hidari Maru*. Fujiwara came out onto the bridge and barked a command over the loudspeaker. The *Tuktoyatuk Scheme* was cast off. I held my breath, certain they'd shoot holes in her.

At first it seemed the schooner would hover beside the destroyer, her wooden hull knocking against the armor-plating. Then she moved off subtly, as if unconsciously. They would wait until she was a hundred, two hundred yards off, then Fujiwara would give the command, the battle bell would clang, the men would scramble, and the motors would gurr as the cannons and machine guns avidly swiveled, fixing on the *Tuktoyatuk Scheme* . . .

The schooner was well away but still lolling with an abandon more foolish than graceful or courageous. Then she turned, no longer broadside with the *Hidari Maru*, and began moving through the water.

They'll sink her—now they'll have their fun! For she was no longer trying to seem offhand and larky, but was running for it, going all out. I gritted my teeth. It was time for Fujiwara's command . . .

In less than a minute the *Tuktoyatuk Scheme* vanished, though I know that's impossible—it's miles to the sea's horizon. But she was very light, unburdened of my typewriter, manuscripts, me. She was pure ship, and popped over the horizon like a fox jumping a log.

I joined the crew for meals in their narrow, low-ceilinged galley which was very much like a bullet's view of a gun barrel. Their voices rang and clattered in this difficult room as they all talked at once. During meals it wasn't unusual for two or three of these men to bang their heads on the table and moo. The others ignored this. Sometimes it happened that these fits of grief would hit at the same time the electricity (a sometimes thing aboard the *Hidari Maru*, and especially capricious in the galley) would wane, reducing the crew to little more than roiling shadows. In the next instant the lights would flash brighter than before and the men who had been overwhelmed moments before, would be again upright and talking as loudly as the others, if not louder, and even breaking into song, their faces intense, their eyes fierce.

I had free run of the ship and found that no matter where I stood on the *Hidari Maru* I was looking at the back of someone's head, and I would discover, by turning unexpectedly, that someone else was watching me! I was on speaking terms with most of the crew, and as the ship became increasingly small, we were always bumping into each other in the passageways or coming out of our quarters. The crew spoke English proficiently though sporadically, and in a brittle, flitty way that made me at times believe they had absolutely no idea what they were saying. When I spoke to them they would usually respond, though I often got the impression from a certain gleam in their eyes that they were reaching far wider implications than I intended. Or I might be speaking to one of them and he would loudly interrupt me—not in English, and not (or so it seemed) in Japanese.

One day conversation in the galley turned to the Emperor's birthday. At a most crucial point the crew went into a howling crescendo and the lights faded. I stared down at my plate, hoping they might calm down and return to English. They abruptly stopped, the lights came up, and when I raised my head, they were staring at me.

One said, "Tell him."

"Joe, you'll be there. On the big day. Fujiwara-san sent the word."

"That's wonderful," I said. "But what will happen?"

They looked away, glancing at each other from under their brows. "Many things," someone whispered. "Everything," another said, turning away. The rest nodded, humming *Everything*.

"I will read a story!" I exclaimed. "How tremendous after all these years to be invited to give a reading!"

The crew went back to their duties, and I went off and began a story for the Emperor's birthday. But my heart wasn't in it—I was distracted. For the first time in my life, I, Hobart Stull, was worried. I went to talk to Fujiwara.

I found him in his cabin facing the seedy fellow who had served as our translator, beneath a two-blade fan which had been installed in the ceiling. As the electricity went on and off, the fan turned hesitantly, once running long enough to actually stir the hot air before it stopped.

It seemed I was interrupting a conference requiring meticulous notes, for on Fujiwara's desk was a flat wooden box of writing brushes, a small stone basin for ink, and a narrow scroll half-covered with writing; the translator balanced on his knees a writing pad and ink well. Perhaps they were planning for the Emperor's birthday. I had come at just the right time!

I stood waiting. The cabin was incredibly hot. I wiped my brow and leaned against the bulkhead by the door. Through a porthole the horizon appeared, then sank. The fan's slow revolutions motioned me nearer, and I heard far off the slow echo of words . . . "What?" I said.

Fujiwara and I were alone. At his desk, he looked off to the side.

"Captain Fujiwara," I said softly. Too softly—I hardly heard my own voice. Louder—"Fujiwara-san, I respectfully request information concerning the festivities you intend for the Emperor's birthday and . . ." My voice sank to barely a whisper. I couldn't hear myself, but continued speaking.

Fujiwara moved. His left hand. A flick of a muscle at the base of his thumb.

I heard myself say, " . . . blue insinuations, oblique . . ." I stopped. "This crew . . . urges me to participate in festivities. I am honored and greased . . . honored and *pleased*. However, dubious."

Still staring off, he spoke at length in Japanese. I glanced over my shoulder to see if perhaps the translator was standing behind me; he wasn't. I tried to make something of what Fujiwara was saying. He slowly turned to me: his eyes were crooked, the left lower and half-again larger than the right. Perhaps the muscles of his left eye sagged in off-moments, allowing the eye to come forth with a deep, motherly sadness.

He stopped. The sea, the ship, the tiny cabin slowly tilted one way, then the other. I said, "Something appropriate to the occasion?"

His head moved and his right eye fixed me. His lips curled and he said, "Yes," as if the word gave him great pleasure. "You are appropriate occasionally."

Though he didn't mean exactly that. Bowing, I backed out of the room.

I was still quartered in the cubicle where they put me when I first came aboard. My manuscripts, stacked to the ceiling, were stirred to life by the subtle movement of the *Hidari Maru* and would come avalanching down. Amid the worst confusion it was impossible to see what I was writing: I would be at one end of the compartment, buried to the eyes, while the typewriter and my hands, surfacing at the far end of the room, would be working on. Even when the ship was steady and the stacks were motionless, I heard surreptitious slitherings, and a manuscript would come sneaking down onto my typewriter. I would shove it aside, and a few minutes later another story, or two, or a dozen, would come looping and sailing down on me. Daily it got worse. From the beginning I had known I was fathering a family of vigorous eccentrics; but now it was clear they had gone beyond that—I was living down there with clowns, jackanapes, a great band of babooning buffoons. But I was writing better than ever before, as if that shifting mountain and all those people in it were calling forth more: we were there altogether, a rowdy, cart-wheeling welcoming party.

Nights I slept on my bed of words, and as the *Hidari Maru* rolled at anchor, the pages under me rustled and small voices called far off. The night after Fujiwara informed me I was appropriate, the voices howled warnings, and with melancholy thoroughness I saw Hobart Stull, his typewriter hanging from his neck, standing before the crew on the Emperor's birthday. Stull smiles his customary sheepish, ingratiating smile, and turns. Captain Fujiwara, with characteristic dreaminess and grand ceremonial slowness, steps behind the author and, putting a hand to the back of his head, leans against him. This leaning is gradual, and is aided by the roll of the ship. Bit by bit, Hobart Stull tilts. Slow minutes pass, while Fujiwara leans harder against the head of the honorary writer. At last Hobart

Stull can tilt no farther. Over he goes, head-first—or typewriter-first. Peering over the side with the crew, we see a silent splash and a great giggle of bubbles rising to the surface, trailing off to a titter, soon gone, leaving the sea as placid as before . . .

Tossing and turning, I stirred answers from the manuscript, gabbles of dialogue sending advice; blurry scenes in which characters intended for altogether different purpose tried to reshape themselves and come to the aid of their little god; and toward dawn there would be a commotion on deck the *Hidari Maru*, a call to arms to save Hobart Stull would erupt into a slow-motion brawl between the crew and my characters, while on the bridge a leopard reared up, showing his white belly, its forepaws on the rail, a captain's cap cocked over one ear, and it smiles down on the struggle from which Hobart Stull slowly vanishes, his machine still around his neck, the last we see of the illustrious pair, the wide grin of the typewriter keys.

This pandemonium showed at least once a night, double-billed with affairs I was inventing for my piece on the Emperor's birthday—for I was going through with that on the outside chance the honorary writer wasn't to be killed. The story I was writing was aimed at satisfying Fujiwara's tastes: it was rife with adventure but laced with love, a combination which of course brought the blights of Hell on everyone involved, concluding with a scene spewing with redemption.

In a few weeks—or months—I finished it and the very next morning, as if these matters were somehow synchronized, the crew came to breakfast in full uniform, a stern and solemn procession, their faces like fists, their eyes bright as children's.

Around the table there was the spirit of hunters ready for the hunt, of young blades ready for the dancing girls. They threw plates, sent bowls spinning across the floor, kicked over chairs, roared with laughter.

The bosun made everyone shut up and sit down. The crewmen went one by one to the end of the table and delivered speeches from frayed little notebooks which they clutched in their hands. Following the speeches, they sang patriotic songs and, locked arm in arm, we went stomping down the passageway and up onto the deck. For the rest of the morning there were games, feats of strength, and music over the loudspeaker.

After an hour or so, the music stopped, the crew fell silent, and following the bosun's lead, they wiped their faces and donned their tunics. Captain Fujiwara appeared on the bridge and, stepping to the microphone, addressed the men with a speech spoken much too loudly: the still white air rang, the deck vibrated, and his words carried miles across the water. The crew shouted *Bonzai!* again and again, and on the piercing silence that followed, the flag was hoisted—that fierce red sun on stunned white.

Fujiwara ordered the anchor weighed, and the ship turned slowly as if floating up from sleep. Fujiwara spoke down the tube, and the *Hidari Maru* trembled within herself. Black smoke coughed from the main stack. A cheer went up.

Hidari Maru churned full-steam through the water, the men silent, holding the rail and leaning into the movement, the wind in their faces.

Five minutes passed. Fujiwara spoke down the tube. The powerful throbbing ceased, the ship fell totally silent, though we still surged through the water. The wind was less strong in our faces, then there was no wind, and we were again dead in the water. Fujiwara nodded. The winch screamed across the sea as the anchor went out.

Then the banquet. But all exhilaration had seeped out. There remained that particular serenity like pained joy which one feels after the funeral of a comrade who dies again and again in memory and goes again and again to receive those judgments and terrific rewards reserved for men who die in war.

The crew went below and I heard their doors shut one by one. There was no wind. Not a ripple moved on the sea.

The crew came up wearing dark kimono and sat on the deck facing the bridge. Fujiwara appeared also in kimono and motioned me to come up. He turned his back to the microphone and said, "Have you remembered everything?"

I was afraid to answer, seeing myself sink through green water, my typewriter grinning like a big-faced fish determined to take me as deep as we could go.

I held up the manuscript. Fujiwara glanced at it and back at me. "My story," I said. "You wanted this, didn't you?"

He smiled his sly and cunning smile. "Only if everything is remembered."

My typewriter took me through cold green water to the black solid water at the bottom of the sea, and that being as far as I could go, I stood calmly before Captain Fujiwara and with the same certitude with which I might write a line across a page, with the same gratifying sense of bringing everything home while at the same time sending everything off on its own, I stepped up, read the title, and by the time I finished the first paragraph I was caught up in the story—caught up by the sound of the words amplified across the sea, and that implacability of things happening as they must.

I read on and on—it was longer than I realized. But I persevered, holding the manuscript closer as the day sank. The crew were indistinct in the slanting shadows across the deck. I read on, my nose in the manuscript; someone set a candle by the microphone.

That night a profound pulsation, a subtle swelling of the ocean, raised and slowly lowered the *Hidari Maru*. Out of the corner of my eye I saw the tip of the moon put first light across the sea, and I realized the *Hidari Maru* was turning slowly to starboard, until the anchor stopped its drift, then moving slowly to port. Each time it was halted, the chain clanged far down.

I was reaching my conclusion. Had anyone listened? Were they in fact still out there? I was certain the crew had slipped off and were at this moment below, sound, asleep, dreaming of the Emperor on his birthday.

The prow of the *Hidari Maru* smoothly cut the horizon and touched the red arch in the east. The anchor halted the turn with a groan deep in the ship, and in the blood that washed the deck I saw no men, only mounds of shadow.

"Is that all?" It was Fujiwara's voice.

My faith reaffirmed, at that point I ended my story and turned to him.

Jerry Bumpus's novel *Anaconda* was published by December Press in 1967 and has since become an underground classic. His other books include *Things in Place*, a collection of stories published by Fiction Collective, and *The Worms Are Singing*, a novella published by Vagabond Press. His stories continue to be widely published and anthologized. He teaches at San Diego State College.

"Jerry Bumpus is one of those extraordinary writers whose imagination is never dull. He transforms the mundane world, writing about subjects no one else would perceive as interesting, not only making them exciting but having the reader goggle at his imagination. Bumpus, like Diane Arbus, understands that the real world IS grotesque and that half of our pleasure in life comes from being able to perceive those grotesqueries in the matrix of their commonality. *Special Offer* presents both the acceptance of every day freaks and the special imagination of the observer. Sometimes Bumpus' imagination is like a funhouse mirror where perspectives are changed drastically. In "On the Emperor's Birthday" the very big reality of the American-Japanese conflict during World War II is changed into a dwarf reality. The bizarre plot, with its surrealistic action and slapstick characters, is typical of his high, wide style of comedy. His vision will shock, surprise, and intrigue you."

—Diane Wakoski